Lizzie,

AGAINST THE ODDS

S LUCAS

S Lucas

Cover design: Peachy Keen Author Services
Editor: BBB Publishings
Proofreader: Proofreading by Mich

slucasauthor@gmail

❀ Created with Vellum

To all the people who believed I could do this, thank you. Without your encouragement, I'm not sure I'd have ever gone the final step. You guys know who you are.

AUTHOR NOTE

This book is intended for mature readers and includes M/M, as well as some M/F scenes. Some readers may find some content of the story triggering. This story contains homophobic slurs, cheating, violence and bullying in some chapters. As part of the Alphabet Mafia, I fully support the LGTBQ+ community.

BLURB

Marcus Brady seems to have it all. He's the captain of the football team and dating the head cheerleader but things aren't always how they seem. When the new guy at school catches his eye, he soon realizes that feelings are being awoken in him that he never expected. Will others accept the new him, or will it all go to hell?

Trey Banks is the new guy at school, starting from scratch with his mom after they move to a small town for a fresh start. Trey can finally be who he is meant to be. Marcus, the jock, is a temptation he never asked for but he just can't resist. Are his fantasies about Marcus just that, or could they become something real?

Soon enough, both guys find themselves fighting against the odds.

CHAPTER ONE

Marcus

Pulling my Jeep into an empty space in the lot, I kill the engine and open the door. Franklin, my best friend since we were kids, jumps out of the passenger seat and slams the door behind him. "...So I'm thinking maybe I can get my cousin to buy some kegs for the party after the game on Friday, he'd totally be up for it as long as I pay him."

Not really listening, I grab my letterman jacket from the back seat and shrug it on before shouldering my backpack. Carefully shutting my own door before hitting the lock button on the remote and pocketing my keys. I look over the roof of my Jeep at Franklin who's staring at me, his elbows leaning on the metal frame, waiting for my response.

"Sure man, sounds good." I can't quite get myself to sound cheerful as I walk to the curb, Franklin following behind me.

"Come on dude lighten up, it's gonna be awesome. We'll win the game, get drunk, screw chicks in the hot tub. Plus my parents are away for a few weeks, on a business trip, so we don't have to worry too much about clean up for a while."

Screwing girls, that is pretty much all Franklin does. He

has a new flavor each week and constantly thinks with his dick. Some of the girls don't even seem to care that he is a basic man whore as long as they get a piece of 'The Beast'.

I'm not even sure at this point what they are referring to with that nickname, whether it is the sheer size of Franklin Goodman, or if it's what lies inside his pants. It could be either.

Pulling me from my own thoughts, Franklin smacks his shoulder into my own.

"Are you worrying about Rachel again? Look, if she just ain't doing it for you any more, drop her and move on to someone else on the squad. Chelsey's always had the hots for you and man does she give great head, not that mine fits all the way in, but damn the things she can do with that tongue," he laughs before grinning.

It's not that Rachel doesn't do it for me any more, I've just not felt as attracted to her for a while. In the beginning, she was the hottest girl in the school and it just made sense for us to hook up, with me being the quarterback of the foot-ball team, and her being the head cheerleader.

My parents absolutely adore her, but they only see the side of Rachel that she wants them to see. Mom keeps telling me what a cute couple we are, how she can't wait until we get married, and that we are going to make beautiful babies. That thought makes me shudder, to be tied to Rachel in that way.

I haven't even thought that far into the future. Right now I'm still in high school. My eighteenth birthday isn't for a few weeks. When high school is over, I want to get out of this town and head to college, and if that's without Rachel, then so be it. My heart just isn't it with her anymore.

I pull my cell from my jacket pocket, opening the text notification from Rachel as I head into the school building. There's a picture of her in front of the mirror, in the reflection she's wearing her cheerleader outfit with her panties in her hand while blowing a kiss.

Guess what I'm not wearing today? reads the message below the picture. Shaking my head I shudder. I quickly exit my messages without even responding and shove my phone back into my pocket. I really don't have the headspace for her right now.

"It's not that man, I think I'm just nervous for the game. It's all good!" I lie, it's the best I can come up with.

"I don't even know what you're worried about Marcus, we'll own the other team on Friday. Like we always do." As we reach our lockers, Franklin goes to lean up against them but stops when Jessica, another chick from the cheer squad, throws herself into his arms.

Franklin grunts as he catches her, his hands landing firmly on her thighs and pulling her against him as she lets out a soft moan and their lips collide.

Turning away I put the combination into my locker and open it, grabbing the books I need for class from inside, I shove them into my backpack and slam it shut.

Franklin doesn't even bother grabbing anything from his own locker, his hands are already a little full with Jessica's ass. He probably won't even pay attention during class anyway. I'm surprised the coach even lets him stay on the team with his grades, but he is one of the best players we have, that's the only reason I can think of.

Leaving Franklin to his bit of action, I start to walk away before hearing a squeal then the sound of his footsteps catching up with me.

CHAPTER TWO

Trey

Honest to God, why in the hell did my mom decide to drag us all the way to this tiny little town in the middle of nowhere? Oh yeah, I remember, because she finally had enough of my dad's bullshit, the constant arguing, and the fact that he can't accept that I am gay.

Her boss had offered her another job, in the same position but one that desperately needed filling in this town, which meant they offered her higher pay than what she'd been paid in the city. That was the final piece falling into place so we could pack up and move thousands of miles from our home, leaving my dad behind.

I probably should have been grateful too, at last, to be away from his bullying, his beatings. His snide comments had always left me more hollow inside than any of his hits ever could, but he was still my dad and a part of me still loved him. Even if he couldn't get over the fact that I was into guys.

I'd tried for months to hide my feelings, at school I'd dated girls, scored a hot as sin cheerleader as a girlfriend, and even tried out for the football team, all the things a straight guy would do right? But still, I just couldn't seem to find myself attracted to the girls I slept with. The connection was just never really there.

I eventually realized why I wasn't interested in the hot chicks last year at my friend Deke's pool party when I stumbled across two openly gay guys from class getting it on behind the pool house when I went to change.

As soon as I saw them kissing, I knew I should have walked away, but instead I pulled back into the shadows, I just couldn't stop looking at their locked lips, and their hands trailing over each other's bare chests.

When one of them slowly dropped to his knees taking the other guy's trunks with him, it was game over, my cock had been instantly hard and straining against the zipper of my uncomfortably tight jeans.

I'd rubbed my hand over the top of my bulge as I continued to watch. He began to lick up and down the other's hard shaft before wrapping his lips around him and sucking him down. Their moans drifted into the air and I continued to watch from the shadows. When his release was voiced, they kissed lazily before leaving.

Pulling out of my hiding space, I ran into the pool house throwing the lock, and moved to the bathroom, slamming the door behind me. When I looked in the mirror my cheeks were flushed, and my eyes dilated. My heart felt like it was going to beat straight out of my chest.

My cock was like a steel rod in my jeans, I quickly undressed and fisted it. Moving my hand up and down as I gripped the sink with my other, it didn't take long for me to cry out my own release and it was the strongest orgasm I'd ever had.

"Trey..." my mom's voice splinters my memory of that night and I find my hand gripping my thigh tightly, "Trey are you listening to me?" She glances at me from the corner of her eye, before averting her full attention back to the road.

"Sorry mom," I look over at her, releasing the death grip I have on my leg and smile. The way she looks at me makes me realize my attempt to put her at ease doesn't quite work.

"Anyway, I was just saying you're going to have to catch the bus home after school." She's tapping her fingers lightly on the steering wheel, a tick she has when I don't listen. She hates having to repeat herself. "My new boss asked me if I could work a little later to cover for Sharon. I promise once we're all settled, I'll take you out to buy a car. Also don't forget I left you some food in the fridge, and please for the love of God get some more of your boxes unpacked."

"Sure thing, mom." The school comes into view ahead of us and I cast my gaze out of the window toward it. For such a small ass town the school looks pretty big, hopefully, they will have a football team that needs a new player.

Turns out that is one thing I actually enjoyed at my old school and I'd been pretty friendly with some of the jocks there, probably why I'd ended up dating a few of the cheer-leaders. Even though we lived in the city no one there was put off by my piercings or tattoos, there were definitely a few piercings my exes said they enjoyed.

As the car pulls up next to the curb, I reach down and grab my backpack and start to open the door. A hand grabs my arm, and I stop, turning back to look at my mom,

"Have a good first day okay, I know you're starting part way through the year and there's going to be cliques already established but please try and make some new friends," as she gently squeezes my arm, I nod before pulling the rest of the way out of the car and raising my hand to wave as she pulls away.

I watch after my mom's car before it disappears from view. Rolling my shoulders, and cracking my neck, I let out a shaky breath before turning to the school behind me. This is a fresh start, okay maybe not one I had wanted or asked for, but back home, other than my parents and Deke, no one else knew I was gay.

I am not going to hide it here though, these aren't people who I grew up with and I am not going to continue to lie to myself because I am scared they will judge me. If they do, that is their problem.

I am just going to go about my day, maybe see if they need any new players on the football team, hell maybe I can find a hot guy to spend some time with. I shake myself out of my thoughts to make my way inside the school building.

CHAPTER THREE

Marcus

"Watch it loser!" Franklin shoves Nate, the brown haired geek, into the lockers before he slides down them, his books ending up spread across the floor. Shaking my head, I carry on walking down the hallway, not even offering to help the kid who is now on the floor trying desperately to gather his dropped belongings.

"Come on Marcus, you gotta admit that was funny," Franklin sniggers as he punches my bicep before slinging his arm over my shoulders.

"Sure Frankie, whatever you say," I shrug him away before continuing my walk to algebra. Shoving through the door, not even bothering to hold it for Franklin, I walk to the group of empty seats at the back of the classroom. Grabbing the one in the middle, Franklin follows close behind me and drops himself into the seat to my right.

The other kids know to leave the tables at the back empty no matter the class, they are reserved just for the jocks and cheerleaders. Running my hand through my short brown hair, I let out a sigh as I start to empty out the items I need from my backpack. High school is starting to get boring. It is the same shit, just a different day.

Dropping my backpack to the floor I inhale sharply, the sickly sweet smell of perfume hits me. Rachel Turner...head cheerleader and queen bee around here. If she wants something, she gets it and she takes no prisoners. And since the beginning of the year she decided she wanted me, the quarterback of the football team.

We'd hooked up a few times earlier in the year and went to all the parties together before she decided she was my 'girlfriend'. Don't get me wrong, she is hot as hell with her wavy honey blonde hair, sparkling blue eyes, perfect tan, and her body isn't too bad either but she just isn't doing it for me any more.

I slowly raise my eyes to look at her, a slight shudder passing through me as I roll my shoulders thinking of the text she sent when I arrived this morning.

"Hey gorgeous," she drops herself into my lap, her ample breasts pressing up against my chest as she loops her arms around my neck. Her rose-colored lips brush my own before trailing up my cheek. Nipping at my earlobe, I let out an involuntary groan.

"Coming to Franklin's party on Friday after the game? I might have a surprise for you," she whispers. The look of mischief on her face tells me she's plotting, but what exactly, I'm not sure I want to know.

I grab her arms and unwind them from my neck. Dropping them into her lap, I lean back in my chair to try and create some distance, she's making me feel so uncomfortable. I quickly fold my arms across my chest.

"Sure, I wouldn't miss it. Maybe you should grab a seat before Chelsey gets here, I wouldn't want you two fighting over who gets to sit next to me." I reply, pointedly.

Rachel doesn't take the hint though as she begins to run

her fingers over my crossed arms, scraping her manicured pink nails over my skin, but I see the flash of anger in her eyes,

"Bitch wouldn't dare, she might be my BFF but she knows you're mine!"

Latching her hands around both my biceps she presses her mouth to mine, her tongue trying to gain entrance while wiggling her butt against my groin. I can't stop the groan that escapes me from the friction to my cock.

Rachel takes the opportunity and thrusts her tongue into my mouth, one of her hands reaching up and threading through my hair as she continues to rock against my dick. A clearing throat has me pushing her away from me all of a sudden, I look past her to an angry-looking Mr. Goff at the front of the classroom.

"Miss Turner, Mr. Brady I think that's enough PDA for one day, don't you? You're here to learn algebra, not human biology," Mr. Goff makes his way behind his desk as Rachel finally peels herself from my lap and takes the seat next to my own, tapping her nails against the wooden desk.

"We have a new student joining us today, he just moved here with his mother from the city," Mr. Goff motions toward the half-closed door, "Mr. Trey Banks..." the door finally opens the entire way drawing my gaze to it as a figure enters.

I swallow hard as my eyes fall upon him; he must be at least 6ft tall, with floppy black hair hanging over his forehead, and emerald green eyes framed by thick, dark lashes with a dab of liner on the bottom lids.

My eyes slowly track past his lips as his tongue darts out and licks over the ring in his bottom lip, then continues down his neck where I can see black ink peeking out from beneath the neckline of his black band tee. More tattoos appear from beneath the left sleeve of his t-shirt down corded muscles before ending at his wrist. I wonder if they are all connected.

Trey Banks, as Mr. Goff had called him, shuffles his Converse-clad feet across the floor and shoves his hands into the pockets of his black jeans making the chain hanging from his pocket clink.

"Please take the seat in front of Marcus," Mr. Goff lifts a hand to point in my direction, I watch as Trey's gaze follows the hand before his eyes lock with my own. Not blinking, I can't stop looking as he makes his way in my direction.

Even as Franklin tries to get my attention from beside me, I don't turn away. My dick twitches in my jeans and my eyes widen. Trey is almost to my desk when he stops suddenly and drops my gaze before taking his seat in front of me.

CHAPTER FOUR

Trey

"Watch it loser," I hear as I enter, watching as a huge guy in a letterman jacket shoves some kid into the lockers along the side of the hallway before taking off after the other jock ahead of him while laughing. They both disappear through a doorway off to the left. Some people are such assholes, always picking on the little guy.

Shaking my head, I make my way over to the guy on the floor and crouch down, "Dude, you okay?" I start to help him gather his belongings. His eyes falling on me, a look of embarrassment marring his features. He begins to rise back to his feet and straighten out his Star Wars tee as I stand back up.

"Yeah...I'm good." His voice trembles slightly. "Jocks love to joke around, ha!" he grabs his belongings from me before stowing them into his satchel, "Thanks...wait you're the new guy right?"

"That's me," I smile as I reach up and run my fingers through my black hair, feeling a little nervous. "Guess in a town this small it's not hard to recognize the newbs." I laugh. At my old school, if you'd wanted to disappear you could.

Yeah, people might know you but there were so many in the school you could easily get lost in the crowds. "The name's Trey," I extend my hand toward him.

"Nathaniel," he goes to extend his hand to my own before pulling it back and wiping it quickly on his pant leg. He grasps my hand in his own finally and shakes it. "So I admit my mom works for the school, she already said you were coming today and asked me to show you around. Your first class is algebra, so guess that's where we're heading." His comment settles my nerves slightly.

Nathaniel takes off down the hall with me hot on his heels, he stops abruptly outside the same doorway I saw the two jocks heading through. Looking through the glass window in the door I gaze inside, my eyes flitting across the occupants of the classroom before my focus zeroes in on the brown-haired jock, not the huge one though but his friend.

Draped across his lap and whispering into his ear, his face partly obscured by her hair is a blonde girl, and judging by the uniform she is wearing she's one of the cheerleaders. His face is suddenly concealed entirely as she moves away and I turn my attention back to Nathaniel, I am just about to question if this is my class when a hand clasps my shoulder making me jump.

"Mr. Goff!" Nathanial looks over my shoulder. "That's my cue to leave, see you after class. And thanks by the way," Nathaniel turns on his heel and scurries off down the hall.

"Trey Banks, I assume?" I turn slowly to look at the faculty member behind me and nod. "Good, good. I'm Mr. Goff. If you'll just excuse me, I'll calm down the rabble and introduce you."

Without even waiting for my response, he pushes through the door leaving it partly open. Through the gap I can now see the cheerleader and jock making out, one of her hands grasping his hair tightly, and my cheeks heat. As soon as Mr. Goff clears his throat, the cheerleader is shoved back.

"Miss Turner, Mr, Brady I think that's enough PDA for one day, don't you? You're here to learn algebra, not human biology," I smirk at Mr. Goff's comment, I mean he isn't wrong. As the cheerleader finally disengages from the jock's lap I, at last, get to see all of him.

Chocolate brown hair, a slight five o'clock shadow, and the bluest eyes I've ever seen. "...his mother from the city, Mr. Trey Banks." Crap that's me, I push the door the rest of the way open and walk inside. I try to look anywhere but at the hot jock at the back of the classroom, my tongue darts out across my lower lip as I struggle to dampen my suddenly dry lips.

Don't look at the hot jock, just don't look at the hot jock, he's clearly straight. I chastise myself. I quickly shove my hands into my pockets and play with some of the loose change I have in there to distract myself. "Please take the seat in front of Marcus," I look to Mr. Goff and follow along his hand to who he is motioning at. You guessed it, the hot jock.

Fuck. My. Life. Our eyes collide, neither of us looks away as I make my way down the row of chairs. I hold my breath until I come to a stop. I lower my gaze away from Marcus and drop abruptly into the seat in front of him, the breath I've been holding at last escaping.

The jock's gaze is burning into my back and a shiver runs down my spine. Pulling my notepad and pen from my backpack I try and ignore it and focus on Mr. Goff.

CHAPTER FIVE

Marcus

Sitting at our usual table in the cafeteria, I can't help playing with my food. With Rachel sitting next to me, she definitely does enough talking that my input won't be missed. As she eats her salad, she runs one hand up and down my denim-clad leg.

Part of me wants to throw her hand off, but I don't want to end up starting a fight with her surrounded by our friends. She's likely to take it personally and make me regret it.

Not listening to any of the conversations around me, I raise my eyes to the double doors, wondering where the new guy is. As if my thoughts summoned him, he walks through the doors, followed by Nate, the brown-haired guy that Franklin had shoved into the lockers this morning.

Typical Nate, his mom is the school secretary and chances are she told him to show the new guy around. Lifting a french fry to my mouth, I try to focus back on the conversation going on at our table, but my mind is elsewhere.

As Nate and the new guy walk by us, I can feel at least one of their gazes focused on my back. I don't know what the deal is with the new guy, why the hell does he keep staring at me? I've felt his eyes on me a few times during our classes before lunch, but I've done my best to ignore him.

On occasion I couldn't help but look over at him, a strange tingle running through my body. What the hell is it with the new guy that keeps drawing my thoughts and my attention to him? Shaking those thoughts away, I turn my body more toward Rachel whose hand has been slowly making its way further and further up my leg.

"...see the new guy, he's kinda hot right!" Chelsey's high-pitched voice from across the table draws my attention.

"Did you see all those tattoos?" Jessica counters, "I'd love to get a chance at finding where else he has them." Franklin lets out a laugh at Jessica, yeah she may have been his fling for this week, but he honestly doesn't care if she goes for the new guy. He literally has a list a mile long of girls lining up for him.

"I couldn't even care less about him, why would I when I have Marcus." Rachel's hand has reached my dick and she gives it a squeeze through my jeans, and throws me a wink. I can't stop the groan that passes my lips, she probably thinks it's down to where her hand is, but in truth, it's because of her comment.

Shaking my head, I push Rachel's hand away from my crotch and back down my leg. "Who cares if he's new? I'm sure you ladies will find a way into his pants soon enough and then he'll be last week's news." I grab a few fries and shovel them into my mouth. I feel a pang in my chest at my own comment but push it away.

"We're still on for the movies after school right, Marcus? It's that new action movie we said we'd go see." Franklin must be trying to steer the conversation away from the new guy. "Plus, you know me, I love spending time in the dark with the ladies." He throws a wink in Jessica's direction, and she giggles.

Smirking I know exactly where Franklin is going with

this, honestly, it wouldn't be the first time he's managed to get a hand or blow job in the darkened theater. Actually, he wouldn't be the only one of the guys sitting at the table who has done it. I definitely wasn't innocent of that one myself.

"Sure man," my eyes drift over to where the new guy and Nate have sat down across the room. Nate is talking animatedly with hand gestures and everything. New guy is nodding along to whatever Nate is saying but his eyes are trained on our table. When he notices my gaze, he smirks before turning his attention back to Nate.

My dick twitches again. I really need to get out of here and head to my next class. Pushing up from the table, I grab my backpack and tray.

"I'll catch you guys in a bit." Ignoring any of the comments following me, I empty my tray and leave it on the stack next to the trash can.

Risking one more look over my shoulder, I see Trey's eyes following me as I make for the exit.

CHAPTER SIX

Trey

Nathaniel, or Nate as he later told me to call him, has dutifully been waiting for me after every class so far. Thankfully it's now time for lunch, good thing 'cause I am absolutely starving. Not just for food either, I want to see more of Marcus.

I've managed to get a few good looks at him during classes. Trying to take in every detail about him that I can. At one point I thought I was going to have to get excused from class so I could go and take care of my hardening cock.

I've noticed a lot of the girls looking my way as I pass too and in classes but they've been so doe-eyed that they haven't really noticed where my gaze actually fell. The girls in the school are pretty hot, don't get me wrong, but I just don't swing that way anymore.

The guys aren't too bad to look at either, but Marcus Brady is like a God among mortals. It's just a shame he's batting for the wrong team, or at least the wrong team for me. My thoughts are so focused on Marcus as I exit the classroom I don't even notice Nate already waiting for me, leaning up against the lockers outside the room.

"Come on, cafeteria is this way," pushing himself away from the lockers he makes his way down the long hallway, after a few twists and turns I spot the double doors ahead of me. I can smell the greasy food typical in a school cafeteria and hear the voices of the other students as we get closer.

Pushing through the doors, Nate starts listing off what I think is pretty much the entire menu of food you can grab in the cafeteria, including all the desserts. As we pass the tables in the cafeteria my eyes focus on the table containing the jocks and cheerleaders.

My eyes automatically fall on Marcus' back as we pass. I can hear one of the cheerleaders mentioning the new guy, me. I wonder what they are saying about me, whether it's good or bad, but then I have to remind myself that I'm not going to care.

Joining the line for food, Nate begins to tell me more about the different cliques in the school, they are pretty standard compared to my old school. Grabbing a tray, I add a burger and fries before picking up a chocolate pudding and a bottle of water. Once we've paid Nate guides me to an empty table by the window, I sit with my back to it so I'm facing Marcus.

His attention is finally on whatever the cheerleaders are saying, which from passing I already know is me. I watch as he reaches under the table and moves his girlfriend's hand from God knows where and shoves some of his fries in his mouth. Reaching for my burger, I lift it to my mouth and take a bite.

"So, there's not much to do in this town but I heard there's this new movie showing? Wanna go see it? I think it's some action movie," my attention is drawn back to Nate, he's moving his hands around while describing the movie to me. For just some action movie, he seems to know a lot about it.

I can only nod as I notice Marcus has lifted his eyes and

they catch my own. I can't help the smirk that passes my lips between bites before I turn back to Nate. Marcus Brady is making me hot under the collar, I know he won't be feeling the same way but I can't deny what he's doing to me.

"Sounds like fun. Tonight?" I think back to my mom saying she was working late tonight, so getting out of the house would definitely be a bonus. Especially if it means I won't be sorting through more boxes, I know they need doing but it doesn't sound overly fun.

Mom wants me to make friends, so here I am making friends. Hopefully, she won't hold that against me when she gets home and sees I haven't touched the boxes.

"Yeah, I can tell you where and meet you there if you want?" Nate has already demolished his plate of food; I've been so busy staring at Marcus that half my burger and a few fries still remain.

"Can I get the bus there?" I'm embarrassed to ask. "My mom has said we can buy a car for me in a few weeks. 'Til then I'm mostly on foot." I notice movement coming from the jock and cheerleaders' table. When I look up, I see Marcus has already started moving away, leaving his friends baffled by what looks like a sudden departure.

My eyes continue to track him as he leaves through the double doors. Only half-listening to Nate again.

"I can give you a ride home if you like? And we can go from there? I'll take this as payment," Nate grins across at me before snagging a handful of fries from my plate. I reach out smacking his hand away before laughing.

"Guess that's a deal then, though I think with the amount of fries you just took that guarantees me a ride home after the movie too." I start shoveling the burger down my throat as Nate collects his tray and jumps up heading over to the trash.

Lunch seems to have flown by, but then again, I've been a

tiny bit distracted. I wonder if I'll see any more of Marcus during the day or was that my last glimpse of him.

CHAPTER SEVEN

Marcus

Classes for the second half of the day just seem to drag. At least I don't have any more classes with the new guy. For that, I am thankful at least. I don't need any more distractions, especially with some of the teachers at this school.

A lot of them are hard asses, the only class I really like is gym where I get to spend time with my friends doing something I love. That and football training of course.

I dump my books back into my locker and make my way outside, Franklin is already leaning up against my Jeep waiting for me. Jessica is wrapped around him, their lips locked together. Honestly, one day it would be nice if Franklin actually thought about something other than girls, but I'm guessing that day isn't today.

Clearing my throat as I reach my car, I press the button on my key fob to unlock the doors. Franklin tears his lips away from Jessica and looks over to me, throwing me a wink.

"I said we'd give Jessica a ride to the diner with us. Rachel and Chelsey left her stranded again." Jessica looks over at me giving me a slight smile. Typical Rachel. Why am I not surprised by her actions? She really is a bitch to her so-called friends sometimes.

"Sure, jump in!" I open the door and throw my backpack on the back seat and climb inside. Starting the engine, I wait for the other two to get in before reversing out of the space and heading away from school and towards the diner.

We always head to the diner before the movies, it's small but has some of the best food in town. It's become a bit of a tradition, we sometimes end up there after games too, but this time, we're having the party at Franklin's.

Franklin and Jessica chatter next to me as I drive, but I just leave them to it. I tap my hands on the steering wheel along to the song playing on the radio and let my mind drift. My mind drifts to emerald green eyes lined with eyeliner and a metal ring through a bottom lip.

Christ, what the hell is this new guy doing to me? I don't even think about girls as much as I've been thinking about him all day. Maybe it's just down to the fact that he's fresh meat at school; we don't get many new people moving to town. I mean, why would they if they can live in one of the bigger cities?

Reaching the diner, I pull into an empty space and kill the engine. I've missed the entire conversation that's been going on during the journey, but Franklin and Jessica don't seem to mind. Probably a good thing.

Piling out, I lock my Jeep and we head into the diner. The little bell above the door tinkles as I walk through. Scanning around, I see the rest of our group already sitting at our usual table. Rachel is sitting next to Jackson, whispering something into his ear as she runs her hand up his arm. When he spots me striding over, he quickly pushes away from her and Rachel gives a little huff.

She might have claimed me as her own, but she certainly isn't mine. While I'm faithful to her in every way, she definitely doesn't show me the same courtesy. Maybe this is why I've been thinking about the new guy today; trying to get my thoughts off Rachel and the fact that she will cheat on me with anything that has dick. Hell, sometimes I'm not even sure if a dick is a requirement.

Dropping into the seat across from Jackson, I can't help the glare I give him from across the table. At least he has the decency to look sheepish, whereas Rachel is sat next to him with a sly smile adorning her face before she blows me a kiss.

Rolling my eyes, I grab the menu from the holder. I'm not even sure why, I already know what I want but at least it distracts me from wanting to punch Jackson square in the face.

Betsy, the joint owner of the diner makes her way over to us to take our orders. She might be the joint owner, but before she married Ted, she was just a waitress here and old habits die hard. Betsy jots down everyone's orders before her eyes fall on me, "The usual, Marcus?"

I smile and nod, Betsy has known me my entire life and my order hasn't changed in all that time, "Yeah thanks, Betsy. How's Ted?" I look over to the window that looks into the kitchen trying to spot him inside.

"He's good, sugar. I'll just get these orders into him and come back with everyone's drinks." Turning on her heel, Betsy leaves the table as chatter starts up between everyone again.

Franklin nudges me and I look over at him with a tight smile. He rolls his eyes, he knows I'm distracted and I'm sure he'll want to find out more later, but for now, he's happy to give his attention back to Jessica.

CHAPTER EIGHT

Trey

Turns out when I am eventually away from the presence of Marcus, I can concentrate more in class. My last class is biology with Nate, and I end up sitting with him in the only empty seat in the class. There are a few other students from earlier in the day here including a few other jocks I hadn't really taken notice of earlier.

Nate and I spend the remainder of the class talking about the movie we are going to see tonight, and he suggests we grab some food at mine before heading back out. When the bell signals the end of class, at last, I'm ready to get away from school. Grabbing my things, I stuff them into my bag and wait for Nate to collect his stuff too.

Following him out of the classroom, he leads me down the hall toward the same double doors I entered through this morning. Only instead of heading to where my mom dropped me, he swings a left and heads to the parking lot.

We stop next to a silver Honda Civic. "Your chariot awaits, good sir." I can't help but chuckle at Nate as he gets in, waiting for me to join him. Nate reminds me a little of

Deke; both with a wicked sense of humor, but also easy to talk to.

Once I slump down in the car, I pull out my cell and send a quick text to my mom to let her know my plans for the evening. I get a *have fun* with a smiley face in response. Pocketing my phone, I give my address to Nate and start tapping my foot along to the radio station that is playing and look out the window as the scenery passes us by.

"So how was your first day? Make any awesome new friends? Apart from me, of course." Nate's comment has me snorting, but I don't pull my eyes from the streets as we pass them.

"You know man, I don't think I'd have made it through the day without you." As we drive down what I can only presume is the main street we pass a small diner, a few students from the school are milling around outside. "I'm gonna need a map or something to get around."

"It's not that bad. Just takes a little getting used to. But I can always draw you a map," Nate deadpans. I don't even realize we've arrived until Nate jumps out of the car, waiting on the driveway outside my house.

Grabbing my bag, I follow him out of the car and start heading to the front door. I'm surprised we actually managed to rent such a decent house so quickly. The paneling is a light blue color, and it has this quaint wrap-around porch, complete with a swing bench. Trudging up the steps, I pull the key from my back pocket and push it into the lock, turning until I hear the click.

Shouldering open the door, I head through it, holding it open for Nate to enter. Once he's through, I let it shut behind him. I watch as his eyes scan around, taking in all the details. Or in this case, the stacks upon stacks of boxes mom and I still haven't unpacked. I drop my bag on top of the boxes next to the stairs.

"Want me to call for pizza?" Nate grabs his phone out of his pocket.

"Sure, get me a medium pepperoni." I start walking into the living room, signaling for Nate to follow. He's already got the phone next to his ear and is talking to whoever is on the other end as he follows me through.

Walking from the living room into the kitchen I reach the fridge and grab two cans of soda from inside before heading back into the living room. Nate's already off the phone and has made himself at home on the couch.

Sitting down next to him, I grab the TV remote and flick through the channels until I find one I'm happy with as background noise. Putting my feet up on the coffee table, I try to get myself comfortable while we wait for the pizza to arrive.

"So, your mom works at the school?" Nate pulls his attention away from the television at my question.

"Yeah, she's the school secretary. She kinda has her nose in everyone's business. Hence you having your own personal tour guide today." Nate lets out a soft laugh.

"Well, you can thank her for me cause I really appreciate it." I give him a smile. A knock on the door has me jumping out of my seat. As I pass, Nate hands me a ten-dollar bill. Reaching the door, I pull it open.

"That'll be $18.50," the pimply-faced guy at the door announces.

"Keep the change." I hand him more than enough and grab the pizzas from him before kicking the door shut behind me. Making my way back into the living room, I drop the two pizza boxes on the table. As soon as Nate opens his box, the smell of melted cheese hits my nostrils making me drool slightly.

I take my position next to Nate and open my own pizza box, pulling out a slice and shoving it into my mouth. Groaning in appreciation.

"Shit man, you didn't tell me how good this pizza was." Nate hums in agreement. Once he's demolished a few slices, he rubs the back of his hand across his mouth and opens his can of soda taking a few swigs.

"Oh yeah, the best in town. In fact, the only one in town. What can I say? This place is small, if you hadn't already noticed?" Nate smirks.

Demolishing a few more slices between us, we eat in almost silence. Occasionally making the odd moaning sound as we watch the TV. When we've eaten our fill, I grab the empty boxes and take them into the kitchen. Nate follows behind me with our empty soda cans.

"So, the girls at school are pretty hot, right? Especially the cheerleaders. I saw a few of the girls looking your way in class." Nate leans up against the counter. My thoughts trail to Marcus as I remember his piercing blue eyes and perfectly angled face.

"The girls aren't bad to look at, if you're into that thing I guess." I carry on pottering around the kitchen, wondering if Nate will get my meaning. I should feel nervous, but Nate seems like the kind of guy who won't care who I'm into.

"If you're not into...wait, if you're not into girls then...." Nate stammers out.

"I'm gay. Girls are definitely not my type." Nate just stares at me wide-eyed. "Hey, means all the more for you right?" I burst out laughing.

By this point, Nate's mouth is wide open but when I start laughing, he can't help but laugh along with me. We finally manage to collect ourselves. Well, at least I got that piece of information out there. I was a little concerned about how he might react. I may say I don't care but I really want to make some new friends here and so far, Nate seems to be the only one applying for the job.

"Sorry, you just don't seem the type. Not that there's

anything wrong with it, but the girls. They're gonna be so disappointed." Nate smirks. He comes around the counter and pats me on the back. "Anyway, we should probably head out, don't wanna miss the movie."

Grabbing my keys from the hallway as we pass, we head back out to the car and jump in. I assume it won't take us too long to get there considering the size of this town. When we get in the car, I sigh in relief at how well Nate took my news. I've only known him a day but I'm hoping we can become good friends.

It's nice to, at least, know someone in this town, someone who will have my back if I need it. Mom will be happy too; all she's ever wanted is for me to be happy and I really want to make a go of it here. With my dad no longer in the picture, I really can see my future brightening.

Now if I can just spend less time thinking about Marcus Brady, that would be helpful.

CHAPTER NINE

Marcus

Once everyone has finished with their meals and paid, I thank Betsy and wave goodbye to Ted before we leave the diner in our little group. I pretty much ignore Rachel throughout the entire meal, choosing instead to start up a conversation with Chelsey.

It's probably petty of me, as I just want to piss Rachel off and Chelsey will probably get the brunt of Rachel's wrath later, but to see the sour look on Rachel's face. Totally worth it.

Choosing to leave my Jeep in front of the diner, we head across the street to the movie theater and pile inside to buy our tickets and snacks. Rachel possessively grabs my hand when we walk into the theater, dragging me all the way to the back row before pushing me down into the seat and claiming the one next to me. I can't help but notice the fact that Jackson takes the seat beside her.

Putting my combo down on the tray attached to the seat, I shrug out of my jacket and lay it across my lap before grabbing a handful of popcorn and shoving it into my mouth. It doesn't take long for the lights to go down and the movie to start.

Franklin and Jessica are in the row in front of us and as soon as the lights go down, I notice Jessica's head disappear from view. Well, that certainly didn't take long.

Leaning back in my seat, I focus on the screen trying to enjoy the movie. I can't help but admit to myself I'm still a little annoyed at Rachel. I don't know what she was whispering to Jackson but I can only begin to imagine.

Closing my eyes, I see emerald green flash behind my closed lids and feel a slight pulse in my dick. A touch on my thigh startles me and I look down to see Rachel's hand slowly creeping under my jacket across my lap.

Rubbing her hand across my groin over my jeans has my dick starting to stand to attention. Earlier today I didn't really want her touching me, but right now I'm not going to say no, not after the pulse I felt in my dick when I closed my eyes.

Rachel's fingers grasp the zipper on my jeans and she slowly pulls it down. Her hand disappears through the opening and inside my boxers. Wrapping her fingers around my shaft, I can't help the moan that escapes from between my lips.

Thank god this movie is loud, and the fact most people are sitting near the front.

Rachel pulls my dick from inside my jeans and the sensitive end catches against the soft material of my jacket, pulling another moan from my lips.

Swallowing hard, I turn my gaze to Rachel, and she smirks, licking her lips. Her hand begins to move up and down my shaft, squeezing and releasing as she goes. She runs a finger over my slit rubbing the pre-cum around.

Turning back to the screen I drop my head back on my seat

and close my eyes again, enjoying the touch and sensations from Rachel. My hands clasp the armrests on the seat, gripping them hard enough that my knuckles turn white. I bite down on my lip, trying to stop the moans that so desperately want to escape.

The sounds of guns firing is all around me, people are shouting to each other but all I can concentrate on now is Rachel's hand moving up and down my dick and my balls tightening. At this rate, I'm going to make a mess of the front of my jeans.

Before I can think another thought a hot mouth envelopes my dick and as an explosion goes off in the movie, my balls draw up and I follow with my own explosion down Rachel's throat. She spends a little time licking me clean before moving back fully into her seat.

Grabbing my jacket, I pull it back over my softening dick and fumble to get it back inside my jeans before pulling the zipper back up. My breathing comes out in short pants as I try to calm myself. Rachel unlocks my fingers from around the armrest and lays it gently on her thigh.

Looking over to her, she licks her lips once more and throws me a sultry smile. Now in control of my hand, she runs it up the inside of her thigh and under her cheerleader skirt.

Remembering her earlier text suddenly my fingers connect with the smooth, naked flesh of her crotch. Forcing my fingers to rub against her clit, I can feel how damp she already is. Leaning forward, her lips brush against my ear.

"My turn...", her voice sounds husky as she whispers the words to me. My mind still hasn't caught up with the rest of my body as she opens her legs further and pushes my middle finger inside her.

Instinctively I start to push it in and out of her, her wetness helping me push it deeper with each stroke. My thumb connects with her clit and her pussy tightens around my fingers. I slip another finger inside her and speed up my thrusts.

Looking up at her, I see she has her bottom lip caught between her teeth. As my gaze focuses on her mouth, I see a flash of metal through another lip. Startled, I pull my hand away so suddenly I hear Rachel growl at me. My jacket falls from my lap, followed by the drink on my tray which spills across the jacket.

"Shit!" Franklin turns suddenly at my raised voice, his eyebrow lifting. "Sorry I need to go clean this." Grabbing my now wet jacket from the floor and ignoring Rachel's protests, I flee down the stairs and out of the screen, heading for the restroom.

When my jacket feels slightly less sticky, I throw it down and lean on the counter, looking in the mirror. My eyes are still glazed, and my cheeks are flush. My thoughts of someone else's lips in place of Rachel's have me shaken. That *has* to be the reason why I pulled away so suddenly.

Trying to shake my confused thoughts away, I grab my jacket and head out of the restroom. When I get through the double doors my eyes track up to where Rachel is sitting, the screen lighting up the audience.

My eyes widen when I find her locking lips with Jackson, his hand up her skirt. Clearly finishing off what I started, she can't even wait for me to return. Swiveling on my heel, I storm back through the double doors and straight into something hard.

"Fuck!"

CHAPTER TEN

Trey

Nate and I chat a little more on the way to the theater; I say we, but it's mostly Nate talking as he tells me a bit more about the town and what there is to do. Or more to the point, the fact there's not that much to do here. He tells me about the football game on Friday and asks if I want to go with him.

Explaining that he usually goes on his own just to get out of the house and away from his mom for the evening. Otherwise, he gets roped into watching some shitty Hallmark movie with her. I reluctantly agree.

I ask him if he's dating anyone, which is a little awkward at first, but I let him know I'm not actually hitting on him. I'm honestly just intrigued. It's not to say that Nate isn't a good-looking guy, cause he is but I've definitely got my sights set on someone else. Even if he is straight.

When we pull into the parking lot and he kills the engine, we exit the car and make our way inside. Grabbing our tickets and a couple of drinks, we head inside the slowly darkening screen and take up some seats halfway back.

I spot the flash of a cheerleader's uniform in the back of

the room and wonder if Marcus and his friends are here tonight.

Reclining back in my chair, I make myself comfortable to watch the movie. Nate wasn't kidding when he said it is an action movie. I think we've seen more explosions in the first ten minutes of the movie, than I've seen in the entirety of any movie before.

We aren't that far in when I wish I'd picked up some snacks before heading inside, leaning over close to Nate.

"I'm just gonna grab some popcorn, want anything?" Nate shakes his head not once taking his eyes away from the screen.

Standing up I make my way out of the screen, the sounds of explosions dimming as I get out of the double doors. I decide to head to the restroom before heading to the concession stand.

Purchasing a large popcorn for myself I head back toward the screen, shoveling the delicious snack into my mouth as I go. As I reach the doors, they slam open and someone crashes into me causing half the contents of my popcorn to launch itself into the air before fluttering to the floor.

It takes me a split second to realize it's Marcus, who slammed into me.

"Fuck!" Marcus' hands fly out to grab onto my arms trying to steady himself. His startling blue eyes, even in the low light, connect with my own and his warm hands tighten on the bare flesh below my t-shirt sleeves for a moment before he lets go abruptly, clearing his throat, "Shit, sorry new guy."

Surveying the damage he's done to my popcorn, all I can do is shrug,

"No harm, shit happens." Looking across Marcus' face, I can see the color adorning his cheeks, and feel the anger leaching from him, his breath coming in short, sharp pants. What has got him so pissed off?

"Marcus right? You okay man?" I reach out to put a comforting hand on his shoulder before pulling away. Most guys aren't really touchy, feely and Marcus doesn't know me so maybe not the best idea. "Wanna grab a seat till you've calmed down." I nod toward the seats I spotted near the entrance.

Without saying a word, Marcus takes off in the direction of the seating area. Throwing his letterman jacket onto one of the empty chairs, he drops down into the one next to it. Guessing he's okay with me joining him, I sit on the seat opposite him, dropping my now half-empty popcorn box onto the table between us.

Marcus leans forward on his seat clutching his brown hair between his fingers, muttering to himself. I can't quite hear everything he's saying just the odd name. Rachel, and Jackson. Rachel has to be the cheerleader that's been all over him, the girlfriend. Jackson, not a clue but I'm guessing one of the other jocks.

"Wanna talk about it? I'm sorry, that's a bit forward of me." Reaching my hand across the table, "I'm Trey Banks, the new guy. Just moved here with my mom." Marcus' eyes flit to my own, before looking at my hand.

I can see the indecision on his face before he lets out a huge sigh. Untangling his fingers from his hair, he grasps my hand in his own for a split second before pulling away again.

"It's nothing, just stupid girls and their bitchy selves. You know what I mean?" I nod in response to him, I know just what girls are like, especially in high school. They can be pretty ruthless especially if they think they are the Queen of the school. Wouldn't shock me if that's what or who Marcus' girlfriend thinks she is.

"High school girls aren't exactly the sanest, that's for sure." Thinking about some of the encounters at my old school leaves me shuddering. I hadn't been in a relationship at the point I realized I was gay, so thankfully I wasn't breaking anyone's heart.

I just found myself avoiding too many encounters alone with the opposite sex. But that certainly didn't stop them from trying, and I was constantly having to let them down gently.

"Sorry again about the popcorn." Marcus gestures to the forgotten box of popcorn on the table. Shrugging, to be honest, I don't actually care. My focus is now solely on Marcus. His eyes trace up and down my face resting on my lips. I can't help it when my tongue darts out and licks across my bottom lip.

Marcus flushes, biting his own lip and looking like he wants to say something else. He stands abruptly, grabbing his jacket.

"I'm just gonna go..." he stammers. Before I can say anything, he's already making his way to the exit. My eyes drift down his back, stopping on his ass.

Groaning I consider going after him, but I quickly dash that train of thought away. He clearly doesn't want to talk, especially not to me. He doesn't know me, why would he want to open up to me about whatever is bothering him.

Grabbing what's left of my popcorn, I head back toward the theater, thoughts of the anger vibrating off Marcus and the way his cheeks flushed before biting his lip drift through my mind.

CHAPTER ELEVEN

Marcus

I've never felt the degree of anger before that I feel when I see Rachel with Jackson. I know she has probably been cheating on me behind my back, but to actually see it openly is an entirely different thing. Rachel has always had Jackson wrapped around her little finger.

Before Rachel and I became a thing, I knew they'd been sleeping together but she told me it had never been serious. She'd apparently been waiting for me to finally come around and say yes to her advances. But I saw the way he looked at her. Tonight had just proved it, there was more there than just a casual hookup.

I suddenly realize I've let my thoughts get away from me and I'm still gripping onto the person in front of me. My eyes finally lift to their face; fuck it's the new guy and I've just sent his popcorn flying everywhere.

Feeling the heat of his bare skin burning my palm, I can't stop my fingers from flexing and tightening on his biceps before I pull my hands away clear my throat, "Shit, sorry new guy." He doesn't even seem fazed and shrugs.

I think he says something but I don't really hear him, the

image of Rachel locking her lips with Jackson flashing before me. "Marcus right? You okay man?" The sound of my name pulls me back to reality; new guy mentions something about sitting down.

Without answering I blindly walk to the seating area, throwing my jacket down and I slump into one of the seats. I don't even notice when Trey sits down across from me, my fingers tangling in my hair as I start cursing Rachel and Jackson under my breath.

I still can't believe she did that to me, she *knew* I was coming back. Why the hell was she kissing Jackson, clearly his hand was finishing the job I started to. What reaction is she wanting from me, or is she just thinking about herself and what she wants? Fuck her.

My eyes flicker to the hand reaching across the table in front of me, "...moved here with my mom." Shit, I missed what he is saying again, my eyes lift to Trey's before falling back to his hand. Unsure what he actually said, I huff out a huge sigh.

Removing my hands from my hair I reach across the table and shake Trey's hand briefly before pulling back.

"It's nothing, just stupid girls and their bitchy selves. You know what I mean?" Of course, he's going to know what I mean, I bet he has girls lining up for him.

"High school girls aren't exactly the sanest, that's for sure." I slump back into the seat, barely registering the shudder I see rack through Trey's body.

"Sorry again about the popcorn," I try to sound as sincere as possible and wave my hand in the direction of Trey's popcorn, he just shrugs. My eyes move slowly up his face, my eyes stopping on his lips. When his tongue licks across his bottom lip they follow every movement.

I can feel the heat rushing to my cheeks, my mind thinking of Rachel not that long ago having her lips wrapped around my dick. I wonder what it will feel like to have that metal running up the underside of the shaft and my dick jerks in response. Snatching up my jacket, I shove it over my crotch and stand all of a sudden.

"I gotta go..." I stammer and storm off, leaving Trey still sitting down. As soon as I hit the cool evening air I take in a deep breath, what is going on with my mind right now?

I feel my phone vibrate in my pocket and pull it out reading the text. *Where did you go?* Rachel! I can't decide if I want to respond to her or just ignore her. It would serve her right after all. I walk back over to the diner where I left my car and unlock it before getting in.

I can feel the anger rising up in me again, I should have marched to the back of the screen and dragged her away from Jackson. I don't like causing a scene, but she would have deserved it. Running my fingers across my phone screen, I try and think how to reply.

Writing a few different messages, some angry, some calling her a bitch, I end up deleting them all. I could write so many things to Rachel, but I know that's probably what she is waiting for. She wants to know that she's gotten under my skin. And I don't want to prove her right; my head is in too many different places to even think coherently right now.

Didn't feel good. Heading home. Leaving it at that I throw my phone down on top of my jacket on the seat beside me. Starting the engine, I carefully reverse out of the space and head home.

Maybe it's better if she doesn't know that I saw. Clearly, she wants to be caught, I'm just not sure if keeping it to myself is better for her or me.

CHAPTER TWELVE

Trey

After my odd encounter with Marcus on my first day, he spends the majority of Tuesday avoiding me, but every so often, I feel like I am being watched. Every time I look up though, he seems to be in deep conversation with one of the other guys from the football team.

Wiping the sweat from my brow with the back of my arm, I continue across the field heading for the locker room. Speak of the devil, I see Marcus and his friends ahead of me laughing and joking with each other. Some of the cheerleaders join the group, the one called Rachel, and Marcus' girlfriend wraps herself around him whispering into his ear.

Marcus grimaces at whatever she is saying but she doesn't seem to notice. He looks over his shoulder at me and the look disappears as quickly as it came.

The huge guy, who I now know is called Franklin, thanks to Nate, grabs one of the other jocks, Jackson, in a headlock and they disappear through the double doors and out of sight.

This is my first gym class at the school, and the gym teacher Mr. Tate has decided today is the day to test out our stamina, making us run laps around the field until we are all drenched in sweat. I stop just outside the doors and try to catch my breath, running my hands through my hair. I've run laps before, and they never left me feeling so hot under the collar before.

I spend pretty much the entire class watching Marcus, so when he steps off the track at the end of class and uses his shirt to wipe his face, showing off his lower abs and the dark spattering of hair that disappears into his shorts, my cock twitches, and I stumble nearly landing on my face.

Some of the other guys laugh and joke about my near fall, but I am more concerned by the visible outline of my cock now showing in my shorts. I manage to cover it by dropping down to the floor and pretending to tie the laces on my sneakers until I get myself back under control.

I shake the images out of my head as I enter the building and push through the locker room doors. My ears are assaulted with an onslaught of sounds; locker doors slamming, guys shouting at each other, and off in the distance the pounding of the showers.

"Hey new kid," I look over to the voice shouting at me and see Jackson with a towel wrapped around his waist.

Don't get me wrong he was definitely nice to look at, he is probably an inch shorter than me, lean but also muscular. His usually spiky blond hair hangs limp and drips water down his face as he reaches up with a towel to dry it, his brown eyes catch my own.

"You probably wanna hit the showers before Marcus uses all the hot water!"

I'm not sure if he is joking or not, I mean the school isn't old enough to run out of hot water, is it? Heading to my locker, I open it and grab my towel from inside before stripping off my clothing and wrapping the towel around my waist.

I can still feel the sweat dripping down my back as I make my way over to the showers. As I step into the steam-filled room my temperature spikes. At this rate, the hot water isn't going to matter as I'll be needing a cold shower.

Making my way into the first stall I come across, I drop my towel onto the low wall and step under the spray. Shoving my head under the water, I close my eyes as it sprays across the back of my head and down my body.

Hearing a noise behind me, I startle turning suddenly. My eyes falling on the steam-shrouded figure across from me, I know Marcus is in here but I hoped he was further away, much further away.

As Marcus steps out from the steam I can't look away, the water from his shower sluices down his body. A few droplets bead on his pecs before trailing down over his abs and down to the neat thatch of hair between his legs.

My eyes follow the droplets the entire way before stopping on his groin, and what I see has me drawing in a sharp breath and trying to dampen my suddenly dry lips.

"My eyes are up here, new guy!" my eyes snap up to Marcus' and I swallow hard embarrassed at the fact I'd been openly checking him out. Marcus wraps his towel around his waist and laughs.

"Hey don't worry man, you wouldn't be the first guy in here to check out a guys dick. Hell, I'm surprised The Beast hasn't tried to measure yours yet." I watch as his eyes drop down to my hardening cock and he lets out another laugh.

"He might even have some competition!" With that Marcus smirks and walks out, leaving me standing there with a semi-hard cock and mental images of his too perfect body. It's like he's forgotten our encounter at the movies entirely.

I look round the shower room, hoping to God there is no one else in here anymore. There is no way in hell I am going to be able to leave just yet. Stepping back under the spray of the water and turning to face the wall again, I lean one hand against it as I trail my other down my stomach and grasp my now rock hard cock.

Shutting my eyes, all I can see behind my closed lids is Marcus' naked body. I slowly run my hand up and down my dick, the images in my mind change and it's no longer my hand fisting my cock, but Marcus'.

Licking his lips as he steps closer to me sending shivers down my spine, I pull my lower lip between my teeth to try and suppress the moan wanting to escape. In my head Marcus is placing soft kisses against my overheated skin, nipping gently on my neck as he goes. Tugging hard on my cock, increasing the tempo.

Imaginary Marcus slowly drops to his knees in front of me, his tongue darting out and licking the pre-cum from my tip. This time I can't stop the moan that escapes me, my breaths becoming quicker and sharper as I can almost imagine Marcus' mouth wrapping around my length.

My balls start to tighten as they prepare for release and I know I'm not going to last much longer. With a few more tugs and the mental image of Marcus on his knees before me with his lips locked around me, I cum hard.

"Fuck," my cum splatters on the shower wall in front of me as I continue to grasp my dick, pulling it up, some of it lands on my stomach. With a shuddering breath, I lean toward the wall in front of me and rest my forehead against it trying to cool my skin. I thought that time at Deke's pool house had left me a mess, but it is nothing compared to how I am feeling right now.

My legs feel weak and shaky as my dick begins to soften in my hand, but I know I need to finish showering to rid myself of the sweat and cum on my body. As I turn and reach for the soap next to my towel, I think I see a shadow beyond the steam, I shake my head. I'm probably imagining it.

CHAPTER THIRTEEN

Marcus

Still laughing to myself as I walk back into the main locker room I see some of the other guys leaving, only Jackson is left and he's picking up his backpack ready to leave. He stops when he spots me, "you coming to lunch? I can wait if you want?"

I shake my head, the water from my hair going flying. "I'll catch up." Jackson shrugs as he heads for the door and leaves. I survey the locker room again just to make sure there really isn't anyone left before creeping back over to the edge of the showers.

It's still steamy but certainly not as bad as it was when all the showers were running and I can see Trey with his back to me, one hand up against the shower wall. *What am I doing?* I'm about to turn and leave when I hear a moan, my eyes falling back onto Trey.

From this angle, I can see the muscles along his back flexing, his other arm pumping in front of him, and his ass cheeks clenching. Wait, is he jacking off? I shouldn't continue to watch but I just can't help myself.

I wonder who he's imagining, is it some girlfriend he left

behind when he moved here? I can't help the stab of pain in my chest, I reach up and rub at the imaginary wound. Am I jealous? And of what exactly?

I can feel my cock stirring and I can't stop my hand from reaching down and rubbing over the top of it through the towel, the friction making me harder. Closing my eyes, I see Trey standing there, his long, hard dick pumping in and out of some unknown chick's mouth as he guides her head on and off his shaft.

He starts to thrust quicker between her lips, a sudden thought passes my mind. I wonder what he tastes like? No, I don't, that's definitely not what I'm thinking. *Snap out of it Marcus, you're with Rachel, you like girls even if it's not her.*

"Fuck" I hear, my eyes snap open to Trey, his cum now coating the wall of the shower in front of him. I take my hand away from my own hard dick and stumble back slightly. What am I even thinking?

My legs try to carry me forward once more, but I see Trey start to turn which causes me to stop abruptly. I need to move before he sees me, his eyes flicker briefly to where I was standing as I throw myself behind the wall, breathing hard.

Pull yourself together Brady, just get changed, get to lunch and act like everything is normal. I head to my locker, grab my clothes from inside and start throwing them on. My hand catches on my still semi-hard cock as I try to do the zipper on my jeans, causing a shudder to run through my body. It grows harder still.

I slump down on the bench and shove my feet into my socks and sneakers when I hear the shower shut off. Grabbing my backpack from inside my locker and slamming the door shut, I race out of the locker room.

I storm out of the locker room and into the hallway. Rachel is leaning up against the wall across from the door, a sucker between her lips. Pushing herself away from the wall, she makes her way over to me.

Rachel stops in front of me, her hand trailing down my chest, her fingers running over my abdominal muscles one by one. Popping the sucker from her mouth she leans forward and pushes her lips against my own, her hand continuing its path to my semi-hard cock, I gasp.

Part of me considers pushing her away and continuing my march down the hall and heading for lunch, but another part of me knows I can't walk the halls with my cock as hard as it is. Ripping her hand away from my groin, her eyebrows rise as I drag her down the hall till I reach the janitor's closet.

Pushing open the door I shove her inside and slam the door closed behind us, locking it from the inside. Throwing my backpack on the floor, I grab her and drag her body toward my own. Slamming our lips together, I thrust my tongue inside her warm mouth.

Our tongues battle as I wrap my hands on either side of her ass and lift her. Her legs separating and wrapping around my waist. I turn, slamming her back against the closed door, my cock rubbing against her crotch making her moan. I drop her suddenly and reach for my zipper, dragging it down and releasing my cock.

"Suck it!" Rachel raises her eyes to my own and licks her lips. I don't wait for her to move, grabbing her shoulders and shoving her down to her knees. I yank her forward by her hair until her lips brush against my swollen head making me moan and my dick grows even harder.

Her eyes drop from mine and she eyes my dick, her tongue darting out and licking along my slit. My breath shudders out of me. When her lips finally wrap around my shaft, I groan and push her head further onto my dick. I run my fingers through her hair, but it feels and looks wrong. It's too long and completely the wrong color.

I close my eyes and see a head of floppy black hair bobbing up and down on my cock. Another moan escapes my lips as my fantasies take hold. It doesn't take long before I'm cumming down Rachel's throat, my grip tightening on her hair with one final thrust.

Wiping the cum from her lips with the back of her hand the lust in Rachel's eyes is evident. "I like it when you're rough. We should try that more often." With a quick peck to my cheek, Rachel unlocks the door and leaves me standing there, my softening dick still hanging out.

CHAPTER FOURTEEN

Trey

Christ, I wish I could just concentrate in class, but my brain keeps pulling me back to seeing Marcus naked in the showers the day before. I've caught his lingering stare on me a few times today but every time he realizes I've seen him he quickly drops his gaze.

Tapping my pen on my notebook I look at the clock, I just want this class to be over. Mr. Goff just seems to be droning on and on, and with my lack of concentration, I'm taking absolutely nothing in. My mind is on brown hair, blue eyes, chiseled abs, and a thick cock.

Yeah, there have been guys in the past who have turned me on, but nothing like Marcus. After getting home from school yesterday, I found myself with my cock stiff again and in desperate need of a cold shower which turned into me getting myself off again thinking of him.

The bell signaling the end of class makes me jump and I rush to throw everything in my backpack so I can get the hell out of there and meet Nate for lunch. As I reach the door, I'm shouldered out the way as Franklin rushes past me.

"Watch it new guy!" his voice calls as he exits the room.

Rachel pulls Marcus past me and his gaze turns back to look at me over his shoulder. There's something there in his eyes but I'm not sure quite what.

Exiting the classroom, I find Nate outside waiting for me again. We've gotten to know each other over the last few days and he's a really nice guy. I thought at first maybe he just wanted to be friends with me because his mom had told him to, but it turns out we have more in common than I thought.

His mom, like mine, is divorced but definitely not for the same reasons. He tells me his dad is a good guy, but his parents just fell out of love. They'd stayed together until Nate was sixteen but had been sleeping in different bedrooms for a while before then.

Throwing my arm around Nate's shoulders, I reach up and ruffle his hair, dragging him in the direction of the cafeteria. I might not have figured out where all my classes are yet, but one thing I can always find is food, even without the map Nate had promised me.

As we reach the doors leading into the cafeteria Nate gives me a little shove, ducking out from under my arm. Laughing I push through the doors and head straight for the line, grabbing a tray as I go. It's pretty much the same food every day so I opt for pizza, I mean who doesn't love pizza.

"Wanna grab a table outside, the weather's good. May as well make the most of it." Moving up alongside me, Nate tilts his head toward the double doors on the far side of the cafeteria. Nodding, I pay for my food and start in that direction.

As we pass the table full of jocks and cheerleaders Franklin clambers on top of it and stomps his feet. Tipping over a few trays as he goes but clearly not caring. I stop, I can't help it, I'm intrigued to find out what's happening.

"Eagles rule, Eagles rule!" his voice screams, others join in his chanting, banging their fists on the tables. Holding up his hands everyone quietens down again. "Party at mine after the game tomorrow night, everyone is welcome! Don't forget your trunks, ladies, bikinis are optional"

Another cheer goes up. I look at Marcus, who is yet again staring at me, and give him a nod. Football and then a party, I mean I can think of worse ways to try and make friends. Continuing on outside I find an empty table under the shade of some trees and sit down, Nate sits opposite me.

"Another Goodman party, what could possibly go wrong?" Nate laughs as he dips a french fry into his sauce.

"So, this is a regular thing then?" I question, grabbing my pizza and taking a bite.

"Franklin always throws parties after the game if his parents aren't home. It's a chance for him to get his dick wet. All the guys do." Almost choking on my pizza, I hit my chest trying to dislodge it.

"Jesus Nate, warn a guy," Clearing the pizza from my throat I go straight back to eating, shaking my head at Nate. "Tell me more about these parties."

"They're loud. I heard the last party they had, the neighbors called the cops." Nate eats another fry. "This time his parents are out of town, so they are meant to be getting a few beer kegs in from Franklin's cousin."

"Sounds like my kind of party. You going?" I wipe my greasy hands on a napkin.

"Nah, they're not really my thing. But if you want to go, I can give you the address. Just be careful, gay or not, the ladies will be all over you." Nate laughs, probably imagining me trying to avoid the girls at all costs.

CHAPTER FIFTEEN

Marcus

After dropping the hint with Franklin the day before to make sure everyone knew about the party, he'd jumped up on the table and announced it to the entire cafeteria. We'd had parties after near every game due to Franklin's parents hardly ever being home but usually with a much smaller crowd so it was definitely going to be interesting.

All we need to do now is to win the game and the party will be even wilder. We pulled well ahead of the opposing team early on, and now we're on the forty-five-yard line and there are seconds left on the clock. This is going to be our last play.

The ump blows his whistle, and the ball is in motion, I catch the snap, looking for Jackson, I can see he's not open. I fake a pass to Riley near the end zone on my right and take off in the opposite direction. The ball is still firmly clutched in my hands. The other team realizes my play and starts to converge.

Taking a running jump over one of the opposing team's defense, I dodge and weave around the players that are trying to take me out. I can feel the air displacement behind me as they miss me by inches, but I just keep pumping my legs, determined to make it to the end zone.

There is movement out of the corner of my eye, one of the opposing team's defenders is coming straight for me. The end zone is in sight but he's coming at me hard and fast. Putting my shoulder down I plow through him, grunting slightly as our bodies collide, but I manage to keep my footing and see the pylon bend as I cross into the end zone.

Shouts and cheers go up around me and my team pile onto me with the ball still clutched firmly in my hands. Several pats on the back and fist bumps later, I pull myself out of the center of the group. Man, I need a shower, the game was hard, and I can feel the sweat dripping off me.

Rachel bounds over and grabs each side of my face before smacking her lips against mine. I wrap my arms around her waist and twirl her in the air. Her giggles sound in my ear as I spin us both.

The euphoria of winning lifts my spirits and even after the shit she's pulled, I can't stop myself from tangling my tongue with hers. Lowering her down my body and back to the floor, she's smiling up at me.

"You'll definitely be getting that surprise I promised you at Franklin's party later." With a wink, she spins away and joins the other cheerleaders as they head to their own locker room to get changed.

"Told you we'd win!" Franklin grabs my shoulder, "Also before the ladies tell you later, you stink!" Laughing he marches us towards the locker room so we can shower before we leave. We all pile inside; we're already stripping wanting to head out as soon as we can.

After a quick shower Franklin, Jackson, and I pile into my Jeep and head to Franklin's so we can make sure everything is ready for the party. When we pull up outside, Franklin's cousin Noah is waiting in his truck.

I've barely even stopped before Franklin is jumping out and heading over to his cousin. After a quick greeting, they start unloading the beer kegs while Jackson and I get out of my Jeep. Grabbing a side each, we head inside and take it straight to the kitchen.

It's weird being around Jackson, I still haven't let on that I saw him and Rachel at the movies, so he's acting like nothing happened. Deep down I'm still frustrated with him, part of me still wants to punch him. But instead, I just pretend it never happened.

It's deathly quiet inside the house, but it won't be for long. Under-age high school students and alcohol will see to that. Mr. Ferris and his wife hate it every, single time we throw a party, but they've only called the cops that one time. Let's hope there isn't a repeat tonight, especially now that we have alcohol too.

After a couple of trips back and forth to Noah's truck, we get all of the kegs inside, checking the time on my cell. I head upstairs to get the spare trunks I left here. Heading into the bathroom, I strip out of my clothes; my brain is a tangle of thoughts.

Will Trey actually show up tonight? And what exactly am I going to do even if he does? Part of me wants to apologize for the weird meeting we had at the movies. I left abruptly and then there is the incident in the locker room after class.

Every class we share, my eyes track him, each and every movement he makes. Even at lunch when I am talking to my friends my eyes seek him out. I'm not even sure what the hell it is about this guy that has me so fascinated.

I've heard all the things the girls want to do to him, and they are taking bets on who can get him into bed first. Even Rachel thought she'd manage it first, but I'm not so sure. He doesn't seem to have a single interest in any of the girls who look his way.

CHAPTER SIXTEEN

Trey

After the football game, I wasn't entirely sure if going to the party is a good idea after all, but my mom says she wants me to make some new friends. Franklin Goodwin, the guard on the football team had dropped the hint during lunch yesterday, saying *all* were invited so here I am. By hint, I mean he stood up on the table in the cafeteria and announced it at the top of his lungs.

As soon as I walk through the double doors of the mansion style house, the music assaults my ears. The bass throbs through my body, making my heart rate spike.

The crush of bodies around me is overwhelming as I make my way through the crowds, trying desperately to find the kitchen. If I am going to stick around, I'm going to need a drink.

"Hey new guy!" looking up at the voice I realize it's Jackson, as he makes his way toward me he grabs a red plastic cup and thrusts it into my hands. Grabbing it, I lift it to my lips and down the contents before crushing the cup in my fist and throwing it into the trash. Jackson slaps his hand on my shoulder, "damn new guy."

"You know I have a name right, Jackson?" Lifting an eyebrow, I reach out to snatch another cup from the counter, deciding to take my time with this drink.

"Ha," Jackson barks, "I know Trey, but you're like the shiny new plaything at school. The vultures will soon descend." Slapping his hand on my shoulder again, just as he says the word 'vultures' a group of bikini clad girls enter the kitchen.

One, I don't knows name yet walks straight up to Jackson and whispers into his ear. A smirk bursts across Jackson's lips, grabbing her hand he makes for the door, "That's my cue to bounce, see ya later new guy."

Watching as Jackson drags the girl from the kitchen, I shake my head. Going to take another swig of my drink, I realize it's empty. I better actually start joining in, not like I'm gonna make any new friends hiding in the kitchen. Quickly grabbing another drink, I push my way through the group of bikini clad girls still hanging by the doorway. A few try to grab my attention, but I shake them off.

Making my way outside I see the party is in full swing out here, there's a group playing beer pong, a game of volleyball happening in the pool, and beyond that, there's a few couples openly hooking up in the hot tub. A few people offer hellos as I pass them; I mumble the odd hello in return.

Flopping myself down on the nearest empty recliner my eyes fall back to the hot tub, stopping suddenly on a familiar head of brown hair, and I know straight away it's Marcus. He sits in the hot tub, his arms braced on the sides and his head tilted back with his eyes closed.

Damn that guy, even just sitting there chilling he's hot. Shame he plays for the other team. My point is proven as Marcus' girlfriend Rachel climbs into the hot tub beside him. Her hands running up and down his chest before one disappears beneath the water, she leans forward and whispers into his ear. Marcus finally opens his eyes and looks at her, his Adam's apple bobbing before he gives a faint nod.

That's all it takes for Rachel to clamber onto Marcus' lap, her back to him as she grinds on his crotch. I swallow hard as I watch Marcus' hands reach around her and grip her breasts through her bikini, flicking her nipples as he does. I shouldn't be watching, but for some reason, I can't tear my eyes away. My tongue darts out to dampen my lips before I take another swig of my beer. I really should have eaten before deciding to down two cups, the alcohol is starting to make my body tingle.

Watching as Rachel reaches her hand below the water, I notice Marcus' eyes glaze slightly. I can only guess what that hand is doing, my thoughts are confirmed as Rachel lifts slightly from the water before slowly dropping down, her lips parting, and her eyes rolling up. My eyes flicker back to Marcus' as I realize his hooded gaze is now locked with my own. Rachel begins to lift herself up and down over him. Clearly, she has no issues fucking him for all to see.

"You're such an asshole Jackson!" a shrill voice rings out and my eyes are pulled away from Marcus' toward the sound. The girl who I saw Jackson leaving with earlier stomps around the side of the pool, Jackson close on her heels. Damn, she looks angry, her cheeks flushed red, and her hands balled into fists at her side. Jackson reaches for her arm, but it is intercepted by another guy I don't recognize from the football team.

The voices get louder as they begin to argue, hell what's a party without a bit of a fight? I stand quickly, I should probably stop these guys before someone throws a punch. Making my way through the crowd that has gathered, I finally break through to see Jackson taking a swing.

On instinct, I lunge forward to grab Jackson around the waist and pull him back. As soon as my arms are around him, his elbow flies back clocking me above my eye. I lose my footing, stumbling back toward the edge of the pool. The momentum of the hit, along with my drink addled brain means I can't stop myself as my foot hits air. Fuck. Thankful for once that I left my cell phone at home. *My mom really can't afford to have to buy me another.* That's my last thought as I hit the water hard.

CHAPTER SEVENTEEN

Marcus

Again my mind wanders back to if Trey will turn up at the party tonight. I know he heard the announcement Franklin made to the entire cafeteria about the party being an open invite. I'm not even sure why I want him here, it's almost like I'm trying to tempt fate.

I haven't been able to stop thinking about watching him jack off in the locker room, every time I do my dick gets instantly hard. Usually with no other way to get rid of it than jacking off myself or using Rachel's tight body. Not that she seems to even care or notice. Just the thought of it, yet again, stiffens my dick.

Reaching over the side of the hot tub, I grab my red cup and down the beer inside. Maybe if I drink enough, I'll be able to make myself numb and stop thinking about him for more than five minutes. When the cup is empty, I drop it back on the side and shift slightly in the water.

Closing my eyes, I tilt my head back against the edge of the hot tub trying to relax, the sounds from the party going on all around me. The jocks are talking about the game, that of course we won. And the cheerleaders chat animatedly about who's going to get lucky and with who. I huff out a breath, I honestly couldn't care less. I'd happily leave right now if I could. But I want to wait for him.

I feel the water around me shift, but I don't even bother to open my eyes. Delicate and familiar hands begin to run up and down my chest, one trails down toward my trunks and grasps my hard dick through the material causing me to shiver.

"Is this all for me? You bad boy, I told you I had a surprise for you." My eyes snap open and fix on Rachel, I swallow hard and nod. It's not but I need relief.

She moves to position a leg on either side of me on the hot tub seat, rubbing her bikini clad pussy over my hard dick. With her back to my chest, I look over her shoulder to the other side of the pool. Spotting Trey straight away, his eyes watching Rachel's movement. If he wants to watch her, I'll give him a show. I'm betting now Rachel is who he was fantasizing about when he was jacking off the other day. *Asshole.*

Running my hands around her sides I latch them onto her breasts, her breathing hitches as I flick her nipples feeling them bead underneath my fingers. Rachel's breath hitches again as she dips her hand back below the surface and slips it inside my shorts before pulling my hard length free. Pulling her bikini bottoms to the side, she traps my length between them and her bare pussy.

Her lips part in a gasp as she rubs my dick against her, her head falling back onto my shoulder as the head of my dick rubs against her clit. But I barely notice as I keep my gaze fixed on Trey's face, wanting to see his reaction as our eyes lock. My hands rest on her hips and lift her body up and down, letting the full length of my dick rub against her most sensitive area. Shouting off to one side seems to distract Trey and he moves his gaze away from us.

I don't even care at this point, my dick is rock hard and

I'm desperate to sink into her, I groan imagining her walls clamping around me. I've never gone without a condom and as much as I know I shouldn't, I'm so horny right now. With the tip of my dick poised at her entrance, I look around, wondering if anyone is even paying attention to us but no one is. They seem to have gathered to one side of the pool where it looks like a fight has broken out.

"Please fuck me, Marcus, come inside me," Rachel continues to moan as she tries to sink down onto me, I can feel my balls tightening already. But my focus is broken when I see Trey lunge to grab Jackson who is taking a swing at Matt.

As soon as Trey has a hold of Jackson, he takes a rough elbow to the face from him. As if in slow motion I can only watch as Trey stumbles closer to the pool, he can't seem to stop himself as the edge gets closer, and finally, he runs out of concrete and falls in.

I push Rachel roughly from my dick into the water of the hot tub. Quickly tucking my dick back into my shorts, I make for the steps to pull myself out. I can hear spluttering behind me as Rachel resurfaces,

"What the fuck Marcus? Get back here! I'm not done with you yet!" I ignore her shrill cries as I make my way to the edge of the hot tub and pull myself out.

I don't know what is making me move so quickly to get to Trey's side but I want to make sure that I am there to help him before anyone else is even given the chance. I want him to be thinking of me and not someone else.

Working around the crowd that's gathered I push myself toward the edge of the pool, to him.

CHAPTER EIGHTEEN

Trey

Resurfacing, I can't help coughing trying to clear the water from my lungs as I drag in a lung full of air. Well, that was fun, not. Shaking my head to try and get rid of some of the water I wince, reaching my hand up I touch my eyebrow. When I withdraw it, I can see blood smearing my fingers.

"Shit, Trey, man I'm so sorry!" Swiveling my focus to Jackson, I laugh.

"Don't even worry about it." I start swimming to the stairs. My progress is slow now that my clothes are weighed down by water.

As I pull myself from the water, I spot a shadow in front of me, slowly lifting my eyes up they track up muscular legs and stop briefly on a slight bulge encased in swimming shorts. I continue my progress up till my eyes lock with Marcus'.

The last time I'd seen him he'd be quite happily fucking Rachel in the hot tub, in fact, I'm surprised he isn't still there. Which only makes me question, why exactly is he here now?

"That cut looks bad, new guy. Come on. I'll show you where the bathroom is so you can clean up." Marcus reaches down and grabs my arm pulling me up the last bit from the pool.

As soon as his skin touches my own, I feel what I can only describe as a bolt of electricity zapping up my arm. My eyes grow wide as I look up to Marcus to see if he felt it too. When he shows nothing on his features, I quickly pull away as soon as both my feet are planted on the concrete at the side of the pool.

"Yeah sure, thanks." Marcus turns and begins to walk to the house.

The muscles in his back flex as the water from the hot tub runs down his body. I follow close behind, people seem to clear the way as we walk, some of the guys throw greetings at Marcus as we pass, ignoring my presence behind him.

My clothes are a dripping mess and I pause briefly at the back door worried that I'm going to leave a trail of water through the house but if I don't follow now, I'm going to lose him.

Stepping inside the house I expect Marcus to show me to one of the bathrooms downstairs, but instead, he moves to the stairs passing a few couples making out. Marcus starts making his way up the empty stairs taking them two at a time. I can't help but watch his ass as I follow behind him still.

When he reaches the landing, he takes a sudden right and makes his way down the hall until he reaches the third door pushing inside, leaving me standing in the doorway.

He walks inside, leaving me where I'm standing and I gaze inside the bedroom. Must be Franklin's room, I muse to myself.

The room is cleaner than I was expecting for Franklin. For some reason I expect him to be a messy slob, but he's fairly clean. There are a few sports posters on the walls and a guitar in the corner. Hmm, another thing I didn't know about

Franklin, he plays guitar. It seems there's more to Franklin than I realized.

"You can come inside you know." I look back to Marcus as he opens the closet and begins rummaging inside. When he returns, he's holding some clothes and a towel. "Thankfully, Franklin lets me leave some clothes here, just in case."

Marcus stops in front of me, passing me the clothes. I feel that same jolt of electricity as our fingers brush against each other.

"You get changed and I'll find the first aid kit," he turns on his heel and heads through the door next to the closet.

Stepping inside the room I close the door behind me, setting the clothes and towel down on the bed. I start stripping out of my wet clothing, not even thinking about the fact that Marcus is only in the bathroom.

He's seen it all before in the showers at school so I can't see why it would be an issue now.

CHAPTER NINETEEN

Marcus

Holy fuck, that is the second time I've gotten a shock from Trey. What the fuck is going on? I busy myself in the bathroom trying to find the first aid kit, I know Franklin has under the sink.

Once I find it, I straighten and place it on top of the counter. Taking a deep breath, I lean on the sink and look into the mirror. My cheeks are flushed and my still damp hair drips down my forehead.

"So, this is Franklin's room, huh?" Trey's voice rings out from the bedroom.

"Yeah, cleaner than you were expecting right," I see movement out of the corner of my eye in the mirror and focus on it.

In the reflection just outside the bathroom, I can see Trey starting to undress. He doesn't seem to have a care in the world that I'm standing just inside the bathroom and can walk back in on him at any time.

"I mean, I don't really know the guy, but he doesn't seem the type," Trey's eyes look around the room as he drops his soaked t-shirt to the floor.

I've seen most of him before but this time, it's without the steam of the showers, and I can see so much more detail this time. I can't help but turn to get a better view. Standing in the doorway, I peer back into the bedroom.

The tattoo on Trey's neck runs down and across his shoulders before moving down his left arm all the way to his wrist. It continues down his chest and to the left of his nipple before disappearing down his ribs and ending.

I spot a flash of metal on his chest and my eyes dart back up to it. Through his right nipple is a black bar with balls on the end that stands out against his pale skin.

Trey's hands move to his jeans and he pops the buttons before lowering the zipper down. His hands hook into the waistband pushing the wet material down his legs to pool at his feet. It's only then I realize he's commando.

I watch as he grabs the towel and starts to dry off. Running his hands over each body part as if he knows I'm watching. Which of course he doesn't, he's not even looked up once since I came in the bathroom.

Unable to drag my eyes away from his crotch I take in the length of him, damn he's impressive. For someone who's had The Beast's shoved in his face one too many times, that's saying something, and Trey isn't even completely hard.

I notice more metal but this time through the end of his dick. Jeez, he really wants to pull off the bad boy look. I bet the girls love the various metal throughout his body. It probably rubs them in all the right places.

I can feel that pang of pain in my chest again as I think of Trey with someone else. Trying to shake the feeling away, I turn my back on him.

My eyes move to his reflection in the mirror once more as he pulls my borrowed shorts up his legs and brings the towel to his head rubbing at his hair. Looking down to the first aid kit, I open it.

CHAPTER TWENTY

Trey

I knew he was watching me; I could feel his eyes burning into me without even lifting my head. Maybe I was drunk, maybe I was just imagining it, but I could have sworn it was true. Marcus "The Quarterback" Brady was totally checking me out, or at least that's what I was going to keep telling myself. Now wearing the shorts that I know are his, I make my way toward the expansive bathroom where Marcus waits for me.

"Sit down," Marcus demands as he pulls the alcohol wipe out of the open kit in front of him. Without saying a word, I move to the counter hopping up onto it, and open my legs, keeping silent the entire time. "This is probably gonna hurt, Trey." My name rolls off his lips in the most seductive way, and I close my eyes imagining that he's saying my name for another reason.

I feel the moment Marcus steps closer to me, the outside of his legs brushing up against the inside of my own, the heat of his lower body against mine. I bite my lip to stop myself from moaning, pulling my lip ring between my teeth. When

Marcus presses the wipe to the area above my eyebrow, I can't help but wince, inhaling sharply.

Tightening my grip on the edge of the counter, my knuckles go white. Marcus wipes over it a few times before pulling the wipe away, his body seeming to get impossibly close. I can feel his breath against my cheek as he inspects the wound caused by Jackson's elbow.

"Sorry to say, but you're gonna need more than a band-aid," I can hear him rummaging around in the kit beside me and my eyes snap open watching his hands as he pulls out a few butterfly stitches. When Marcus straightens, he is directly in front of me again and I can see the look of concentration on his face as he pushes the cut together gaining a hiss from me, and lays two of the paper strips over the cut.

"Thanks," it's all I can muster, with the strips finally in place his eyes fall to mine. Marcus makes no move to step away from me as I slide down from the counter. My legs brushing against his as our crotches end up in almost perfect alignment.

At this proximity and with us standing toe to toe, I notice that he's only a few inches taller than my own 6 feet. Tilting my head back ever so slightly, this close I can see the flecks of silver through the blue. His pupils grow wider as I hear his quickening breaths.

It's now or never Trey. I slowly raise my hands, my fingers brushing against his arms causing a shiver to run through Marcus' entire body. He still makes no move to back away, his eyes bouncing between my eyes and my lips. Reaching one hand behind his head, I twist my fingers through his hair, pulling his lips to my own.

As soon as our lips connect a flash of heat races through my body, I expect him to push me away, but he doesn't. Instead, Marcus' hands grab my waist pulling me closer till our bodies are flush with one another. My cock instantly hardens, and I can feel his own pushing against his swim shorts, rubbing together as we both let out a breathy moan.

Marcus' tongue darts out of his mouth, running across my bottom lip, teasing my lip ring, and asking for entry. When I part my lips, he thrusts his tongue into my mouth. Both of us are battling for domination over the kiss, but neither of us is quite getting there.

CHAPTER TWENTY-ONE

Marcus

As Trey's lips connect with my own it's like nothing I have ever felt before, the best way to describe it is like fireworks. It feels like a million volts of electricity shoot through my body all at once. My fingers tighten on his waist, digging into the skin hard enough to leave bruises.

My cock twitches against Trey's as we both moan; pushing out my tongue, I run it across Trey's lower lip feeling the cool metal of his lip ring rubbing against the tip. I wonder what it would feel like to feel the metal against my length as he wraps his lips around my dick.

Taking the opportunity that Trey gives to me, I thrust my tongue between his lips as our tongues collide. Rubbing my dick against Trey's steel length my entire body shudders, feeling myself once again close to climax as my balls tighten. Who'd have thought a kiss could turn me on so much.

The sharp tugs on my hair bring me that much closer to spunking in my own shorts as Trey fights me for control of our kiss. But I refuse to back down, pulling back slightly. I thrust forward grinding my cock even harder against Trey and I feel him falter.

Not to be outdone Trey shoves his free hand down the front of my shorts, fisting me. The heat from his hand sears my skin and I shudder again. This should feel so wrong, but right now it feels so right. Trey's lips leave my own and start to trail down my neck leaving wet kisses till he reaches where my shoulder meets my neck.

Tilting my head to the side to give him better access I feel his blunt teeth graze across my skin before he sucks on it gently. He hasn't even moved his hand yet, why won't he move it? I pull back my hips as my cock pulls back from his fist before thrusting forward again.

Pulling back and forth in his closed first I can feel myself starting to teeter on the edge of insanity. Trey's hand on my cock, and his mouth sucking on my neck are becoming too much. My eyes slide closed as I try to take in every sensation, which is quickly taking over my body.

"MARCUS! TREY!" Franklin's loud shouts followed by banging on the door have me coming back to my senses. My eyes snap open and I slip back away from Trey. His hand releases my still hard cock, and his saliva begins to run down my neck. "You guys in there?!"

Panic seizes me at the prospect that Franklin could walk in at any second, Trey makes to step forward, his hand reaching for my arm. Before he can touch me, I shove him hard, he stumbles back, his ass hitting the counter.

"The fuck man, stay the fuck away from me you queer!" I see the minute my words hit him, the hurt shining through his eyes. I have to get out of here, I have to get away from him. I storm out of the bathroom, readjusting my hard cock as I go. Part of me wants to turn back and apologize but I know I can't.

Grabbing my backpack as I pass, I latch onto the bedroom door handle. I rip the door open and come face to face with Franklin, "Sorry dude." Shoving past him, I don't say anything else as I take off across the hallway and down the stairs. I can hear Franklin grumbling something behind me, but I don't care what he has to say.

CHAPTER TWENTY-TWO

Trey

Still leaning on the counter, I raise my fingers to my lips, I can still feel them tingling from the kiss we shared. And holy fuck what a kiss it was. His final words before storming away sting though, the hurt running all the way to my heart. The rejection hurts more than I can say.

I don't know what the fuck I was thinking when I laced my fingers through his hair and pulled him toward me. I'd just gone for it, the alcohol in my system clearly lowering my inhibitions for that split second.

What I hadn't expected was for him to kiss me back with such ferocity. Since meeting him I'd thought of nothing but him. I'd spent night after night jerking off, imagining his lips wrapped around my cock. The intensity of my orgasms had been off the charts.

My body is trapped between a state of horniness and hurt. Rubbing my hand over my heart, wanting to rub away the toxicity of Marcus' words. I'm so wrapped up in my own head, I don't even hear Franklin approach.

"You good dude?" Franklin's voice startles me back to reality. "That was one hell of an elbow you took." Turning to him,

I wonder if he can see the heat in my cheeks. Pushing away from the counter, I give him a weak smile.

"I'm all good, thanks to Marcus." I point to the butterfly stitches above my eyebrow.

Franklin clamps a hand on my shoulder, leading me from the bathroom and through his bedroom. I quickly grab my wet clothes from the floor and bundle them up under my arm. As soon as I stand Franklin's hand is back on my shoulder. I know I'll have to find a way to return Marcus' clothes to him after the weekend. That's if he's even talking to me by then.

"You seem like a cool guy Trey. You should hang with us some more." Nodding to Franklin, I give him a weak smile.

"Maybe..." I don't even know what else to say to that. I'm not sure at this point if Marcus would even want me around him and his friends.

Wishing I had Marcus' number so I could text him to apologize for my behavior, but I remember it wasn't all me; he kissed me back. That thought keeps running through my head. I've seen him with Rachel throughout the week at school, and even at the game when they won, I made up my mind that he is as straight as they come.

But after what just happened, the stiffness of his cock as I'd wrapped my fingers around him was telling me differently. Franklin is chattering next to me, something about trying out for the football team, and about some girl he planned on plunging "The Beast" into later. But his words are just going in one ear and out of the other.

We walk down the stairs together and Franklin leads me into the kitchen, he hands me another red cup full of beer and I just stare at it. I unquestionably should not be adding any more alcohol to my system right now, my emotions are all over the place.

"I think I'm just going to head home. Great party though

Franklin." Placing the cup back on the counter, I walk out of Franklin's house. I spot Marcus' Jeep parked in the driveway across the street and consider heading over there instead to apologize.

But what exactly would I say to him? *Hey man, sorry I kissed you and grabbed your dick.* Shaking my head I laugh at my own stupid thoughts, the fact he called me a queer means he probably doesn't want my attention. Hell, the alcohol was probably what made him kiss me back, or maybe I was just imagining what I wanted to happen.

Glancing back to the house across the street, I spot a bikini clad female making her way down the drive, from what I can see in the streetlights I think it's Rachel. I want to follow but I manage to stop myself just as I step off the sidewalk to cross the street.

Marcus decidedly didn't want me, not if Rachel is heading to his place. Had he been pranking me? Trying to get something on me so he could spread it around school? Or use it against me? *Come on Trey, stop thinking up so many crazy theories while intoxicated. Walk back into town and call a cab and go home.*

With a plan in mind, I turn in the direction of the main street in this tiny little town.

CHAPTER TWENTY-THREE

Marcus

I don't even know what the fuck just happened. One minute I was cleaning and dressing the cut above Trey's eyes, the next minute our lips were locked, and I couldn't get enough of him.

Walking across the street and back to my house, I test the front door. It's unlocked so I walk inside and retrieve my cell before dropping my backpack onto the floor in the hallway.

The house is quiet so I can only assume my mom and dad have gone to bed. Heading into the kitchen, I pick up a glass and fill it to the brim with water before guzzling it down. Even after the walk across the street, my skin is still heated.

My hard dick is still straining against my shorts and I know there's no way in hell I'm going to get any sleep in this state. I'm too worked up. I move quietly through the house and out of the back door heading for the pool house.

Walking inside I shut the door behind me and walk over to the couch, flopping down. My dick is so uncomfortable right now, I know it won't take me long to get off especially if I'm thinking about him. Rubbing my hand over the fabric on top of my dick, I moan.

Pushing my shorts down my hips, I take my dick into my hand and start moving it up and down. I'm thinking of that kiss. It was hot as fuck, and I want more. Shaking my head, I try and disperse those thoughts.

I'm straight, I'm straight, I'm straight I tell myself over and over again, trying to bring up images of Rachel, or any girl, but all that does is make my dick softer. I could just text Rachel, tell her to get her ass over here. I can't imagine she'd say no, wanting me to finish what we started in the hot tub.

Grabbing my phone from the seat next to me, I fire over a quick text telling her where I am and wait. Closing my eyes, I tighten my grip on my dick, Trey's face is conjured and I'm back to being as hard as steel. Pumping my dick up and down, my breathing quickens.

I don't hear the door as it opens and closes softly, or the click of the lock.

"You're not meant to start without me," Rachel's voice shocks me back to reality, and I'm on my feet in an instant.

Letting my shorts drop to the floor, I step out of them and stalk toward her, my hand still wrapped around my dick. I stop just short of her, letting go of my length and shoving her against the wall, she gasps.

Running my hands around her back, I untie her bikini top and let it drop to the floor. Reaching for her breasts I tweak her nipples, pushing my length against her clothed pussy. A moan escapes her parted lips and I shove my mouth against hers, devouring her.

My hand trails down her stomach to her bottoms and I slip it inside. Her pussy is shaved, and the skin is soft under my fingertips. When I reach her folds, she's already wet, my dick twitches. This is what I want. To prove to myself I'm straight and if my dick has anything to say about it then I definitely am.

I let my fingers run through her juices, coating them

before pushing inside her. Rachel lets out a throaty moan, pushing herself down onto my fingers trying to take me deeper. This is what she wanted at the movies, so I'll give it to her.

Rachel undoes her bottoms and lets them slip to the floor, when she breaks the kiss and looks at me her gaze is heated, and she runs her tongue over her lips. That lip ring flashes across my mind again and I stop all movement.

Fuck Marcus, pull yourself together. I reach into the side drawers next to the door and pull out a condom. Ripping the foil packet open with my teeth, I sheath my dick inside it. Grabbing her shoulders, I spin her and shove her against the wall.

Still palming my dick, I guide it to her entrance and slam home. Our moans echo through the room as I pump in and out of her slick channel. I'm so horny right now, her pussy tightening around me, is pushing me closer and closer to the edge.

Pulling her hips back to meet my thrusts, I sink deeper into her. We've never fucked like this before, usually we're face to face, and I let her ride me but I don't want to see her face right now. I just want to come. Her moans are coming closer together and I know she's close and I arch my body over hers.

"Play with your clit." I whisper against her ear. She tries to turn to kiss me but I pull away again. Rachel gasps as her fingers connect with her nub and her whole channel tightens as she cums. I close my eyes.

Chasing my own release, I continue to ram into her, the slapping sounds increasing and my tightening balls slap against her mound. With a roar, I finally let go but it's not Rachel I'm imagining fucking any more behind my closed lids.

Leaning one hand on the wall next to Rachel my softening

dick slips from her channel. Our chests are heaving as we try and catch our breath and she's got both hands on the wall trying to support herself. Stepping away I remove the condom and drop it into the trash.

"You can leave now," my tone is harsh, but I don't even care. Rachel turns to face me, a look of confusion marring her face.

"I thought maybe I could stay the night. We could sleep out here, do this a few more times." The hope shines through her eyes, but I shrug.

"Nah, I'm good. See you later Rachel." Grabbing my shorts from the floor I pull them back on and snatch up my phone. Unlocking the door to the pool house I walk back to the main house leaving her naked, staring after me. Once I'm back inside the house, I lock up and head to bed.

CHAPTER TWENTY-FOUR

Trey

Banging on the door pulls me from fitful sleep, squinting, I try to open my eyes, but the sun makes them hurt so I close them again. Throwing my arm over my eyes, I try to block out the light, groaning.

"I'll get it," my mom calls up the stairs.

Rolling over, I pull the sheets over my head trying my hardest to get rid of the light. My head is throbbing, and my mouth is dry. *I'm never drinking again.* There's a light knock on the door and I groan again.

"Trey." Nate's voice sounds from the other side of the door. Oh man, did we have plans? I can't remember, my head is too fuzzy. The door pushes open and Nate slips inside. "Getting up any time soon? It's past noon."

"Can you keep it down?" I roll onto my back and groan again. Nate's laughter is like a hammer to my skull.

"So, the party went well I take it." Nate drags the sheet from the upper part of my body; I grasp for it but it's too late.

"It went as well as it could." I try opening my eyes again, staring up at the ceiling above me. If anything, I need a shower. Pushing up I glance up at Nate, the huge grin on his face tells me I most likely look as good as I feel.

"Well drag your sorry ass into the shower and you can tell me all about it. Your mom said she would make us some lunch before she goes to work."

Nate holds out his hand to me and I take it, he pulls me out of bed to my feet and I wobble. Steadying me, he drags me to the bathroom and pushes me inside before shutting the door. I don't even bother to turn the light on as I stumble to the shower.

Turning it on, I step under the water before it's even heated and shiver. Closing my eyes, I let the water cascade over my face. When I close them, I see Marcus in the bathroom at Franklin's, his eyes heated and glazed. His lips fit over mine so perfectly.

Shuddering, I try to stop the stray thoughts of his lips and his hard cock digging any deeper into me. My hangover does not need an erection to go with it, especially not with Nate waiting in my bedroom. Grumbling, I start washing the previous night away, the smell of the chlorine from the pool still lingers on my skin even now.

Pushing my hair back from my eyes, I rinse the shampoo from my hair and let the soap wash away from my body. The soap catching my cut makes it sting. When I finally think I'm clean enough and my head is decidedly clearer, I turn off the shower and step out.

Grabbing a towel from the rack, I wrap it around my hips and use another to towel dry my hair. Walking out of the bathroom I find my bedroom empty, guessing Nate has gone downstairs to help my mom sort lunch.

Opening the drawers I pull out a clean pair of boxers and some shorts, throwing the towels in the hamper I spot the clothes Marcus let me borrow and throw them in as well.

Leaving my bedroom, I head down the stairs and into the

kitchen. My mom and Nate are talking animatedly as they plate up some sandwiches. When my mom spots me, she smiles and walks over, kissing my cheek.

"I wondered if I was going to see you today. Nate helped me make some sandwiches and there's a glass of water and some Tylenol on the counter. Make sure to hydrate today." Nodding, I realize just how easy going my mom is. She doesn't agree with under-age drinking, she'd prefer it if I didn't do it, but she wouldn't totally leave me to suffer the consequences. "Thanks for the help Nate, I'll see you both later."

Pushing me toward one of the stools, she grabs her purse and keys from the table and leaves us alone. Nate is already sat down munching on his sandwiches, drinking a glass of soda.

"So, tell me everything." Ignoring him I quickly stuff the sandwich into my mouth. What can I tell him? I can't tell him about my kiss with Marcus. "Come on Trey, don't leave me hanging."

"It was interesting, Jackson nearly punched someone. I got in the way and ended up in the pool. You know how it goes." I smirk.

"Having never been to one of Franklin's parties, I actually don't." Nate takes another bite of his sandwich.

"Well, you didn't miss too much, also I ended up with this." Pushing my hair back from my forehead, I show him the butterfly stitches above my eye.

"Maybe next time, duck." Nate chuckles, "It's a good thing your mom didn't see that."

Shrugging I go back to my sandwich, when both our plates are empty, I grab them and put them in the sink to wash later. Walking into the living room Nate follows me.

"Please say we can just chill and watch movies, I really

don't have the energy for much else." Dropping down onto the couch, I grab the TV remote.

"Sounds perfect."

Nate and I spend the day doing exactly that, watching movies and ordering pizza from the same place he ordered from earlier in the week. Thanks to some painkillers and several glasses of water my hangover eventually subsides but I feel exhausted.

When my mom gets home from work, Nate decides to head home. I have some homework that I need to catch up on before school on Monday, so I head up to my room to get it done.

It doesn't take long before I start to lose concentration and my mind wanders back to Marcus and that kiss again. He left in a hurry the night before, and with harsh words spilling from his lips.

But maybe that was just because he was worried about what Franklin would have said if he caught us. Maybe the kiss was just because of the alcohol. I'm so conflicted about what happened. I just need to know why it happened.

With that thought in mind, I close my books and head to bed early. I'll have to give Marcus his clothes back on Monday, so hopefully, I can ask him about it then.

CHAPTER TWENTY-FIVE

Marcus

The rest of the weekend is rough. I'm hungover when I wake up on Saturday and as I shower, I keep replaying what happened at Franklin's party. Thoughts of Trey's lips on me leave me hard more than once. Each time, I've had to chase my own release.

I've ignored every call and text I've received, whether it was from Franklin himself, or Rachel. I don't have time for Rachel's shit, and I'm sure if I'd actually answered she would have given me hell for kicking her out straight after we'd fucked.

But I don't care, she'll get over it eventually. My parents are away for the weekend and left early this morning, so I spend my time lounging by the pool. The weather is still nice and I take full advantage of it. Swimming laps and working out in our home gym, I work myself to exhaustion.

That night I dream of Trey, but in my dreams, we aren't interrupted by Franklin. Trey drops to his knees, wrapping his mouth around my stiff dick, and sucks until I cum. I sleep in fits and starts, each time dropping back into my hot dreams.

Most of the time it is Trey giving me a blow job, but on

the odd occasion, it's me on knees, my mouth encasing his steely length, one hand playing with his balls as he tugs on my hair.

I wake the next morning with a raging hard on and I work myself with my hand until my cum is painted across the shower wall. I spend the day again swimming or working out in the gym, calling for pizza so I don't have to cook.

Someone knocks on the door on Sunday evening after my pizza has arrived, but I choose not to answer it. After a few tries whoever it is finally leaves. Taking my empty pizza carton into the kitchen, I decide on an early night. Dragging myself upstairs, I strip off as I go, throwing my t-shirt on the bed. I collapse onto it, and I'm asleep before my head even hits the pillow.

When I open my eyes, I'm in the pool house, Trey is on his knees before me. His mouth moving up and down my dick. My hands are tangled in his hair as I thrust myself up into his mouth. My dick hitting the back of his throat, and his lip ring teases the underside.

Pulling away from me, he rises to his feet. He's completely naked, just how I saw him the night of the party. The bar through his nipple glints in the light. Trey takes my hand and pulls me up from the couch, walking me through to the bedroom.

He pushes me down onto the bed and I fall onto my hands and knees, looking back at him over my shoulder. He opens the bottle of lube that appears in his hands and slicks the fluid up and down his dick before rubbing it around my ass hole. Grabbing my own dick, I start working my hand up and down.

A finger pushes against the tight ring of muscle and I moan at the sudden intrusion. Breathing deeply, I try to relax my muscles, his finger slips inside helped along by the lubrication coating his fingers. He works his finger in and out before adding another, and I watch him over my shoulder the entire time.

Trey pulls his fingers from my ass and I whimper, I want so badly to cum. When I feel his dick pushing against me, I bring my hips back toward him, gritting my teeth, my hand going faster on my own dick. The head of his dick pushes into me and I groan, my dick exploding with my release.

Waking with a start my hand is still gripped around my softening length. To my surprise, cum coats my belly. Releasing my dick, I grab the t-shirt from beside me to wipe up the mess I've made. That was more than a horny dream, I've not had a wet dream since I first hit puberty and not one where I've given myself a hand job while I've been asleep.

Rushing to the shower, I rinse away the cum staining my skin. I really need to get Trey out of my head. I'm not gay, I know I'm not. Fucking Rachel on Friday proved that. But these dreams and thoughts featuring Trey are getting me hornier than I've ever been.

After my shower I dress quickly, realizing I'm running late. High tailing it out of the house, Franklin is already waiting for me. He looks me up and down but says nothing as we jump into my Jeep. We drive to school in silence. Walking in with Franklin, the silence continues.

Leaving me as soon as we walk through the doors, he heads over to where Jackson is standing with Jessica and Chelsey. Glancing over at the group it looks like the guys have swapped girls this week. Jessica wraps herself around Jackson and Chelsey sidles up to Franklin who throws his arm around her shoulders.

Shaking my head, I make my way over to my locker, spotting Trey across the hall. I don't have time for him, not after what happened on Friday night and what then followed throughout the weekend. A tap on my shoulder has me turning.

"I brought your clothes back, my mom...." holding up my hand, I silence Trey's words, and he looks at me with those emerald green eyes.

"The fuck man, can't you just leave me alone. I don't need your kind near me." My words are harsh, and Trey's face drops for a split second before he just holds the bag out to me. Snatching it, I turn my back on him. I'm angry, but not at him, only at myself.

"Sorry." I can hear the hurt in his voice, and I want nothing more than to turn around and apologize, even tell him he's not the one who should be sorry. Hearing his feet as they shuffle away, I shove the clothes into my locker, slamming it shut.

"Marcus!" Rachel's voice goes through me like nails on a chalkboard, turning to her I try to smile. "I hope you're in a better mood today."

Moving up beside me she lays a hand on my arm and I try and suppress the shudder it causes, but I can't, and she feels it. Choosing to ignore it she grabs the back of my head and pulls my lips down to hers, clawing at my arms but I push her away.

"Rachel, can you just leave it?" Stepping back from her, I turn on my heel and stomp off to class.

Classes drag on through the day, Rachel keeps trying to talk to me but each time I find any excuse to leave. Franklin eventually catches up with me after school, he's leaning up against my Jeep waiting on a ride home.

"It's your birthday this weekend, I'm thinking we could have a party at mine. Still got the place to myself." More parties, that's all I need. It is my 18th though, the last birthday I'll have while still at high school.

"I'll think about it." Climbing into my Jeep I wait for Franklin to join me before starting the engine. As I reverse out of the space, I see Trey exiting the building, his eyes lock with mine briefly before I turn away.

Leaving school behind for another day, I have no idea what the rest of the week is going to bring but I'll just have to face it as it comes. Maybe a party is a good idea. It'll be something to look forward to and a way to get Trey out of my mind.

"You know what, a party sounds like a great plan. I'll leave it in your capable hands." Franklin whoops from beside me and I can't help laughing.

CHAPTER TWENTY-SIX

Trey

School had been hell since my brief meeting with Marcus on Monday to give him back the clothing he let me borrow at Franklin's party. He's avoided me like the plague since. If I got too close he hightails it outta there like the hounds of Hell were snapping at his heels. But he still hasn't outed me.

I'm not sure how I feel about that, I decided when I started this new school, I didn't care what people thought about my sexuality. I'd kept it secret at my old school, only Deke and my parents knew, but this was a new start for me.

It's a small town, maybe they won't accept my being gay, but I won't know until it comes to pass. The school definitely has its cliques, and so far I haven't come across anyone who isn't straight. Well apart from Marcus, but I'm not even sure which box he fits into.

Walking through the hall toward the cafeteria I pull the strap of my backpack tighter. My fist clenching and unclenching around the strap. Walking past the group of cheerleaders, my eyes lock with Rachel and she sneers at me.

Did Marcus tell her about what happened between us?

Why else would I get that reaction from her? Trying to ignore it, I push through the doors into the cafeteria, my gaze scanning the room looking for Nate. He's sitting alone at the same table we sat at last week.

When he spots me, he smiles and waves. Heading for the line, I grab a tray. I'm not even hungry but I know I need to at least try to eat something. Grabbing a sandwich and a can of soda, I pay and make my way over to Nate.

Slumping down on the seat across from him, I drop my tray on the table and drop my backpack on the seat next to me.

"What's eating you?" Nate looks at me over the top of his burger.

"It's nothing, classes are just kicking my ass." Not wanting to tell him the true reason behind my silence, I give the next best excuse.

"Have you heard it's Marcus' birthday this weekend, Franklin's holding him another party. You going?" Nate's eyebrows raise when I shrug.

"I'm not sure Marcus would want me there, an after-game party is one thing but his actual birthday is another." Throwing my half-eaten sandwich down on my plate, I push the tray away and sip on my soda.

Grabbing my tray and backpack, I stand abruptly, shocking Nate. Throwing my leftovers in the trash, I make my way out of the cafeteria leaving Nate behind. Walking out of the double doors, I walk straight into something solid, stopping me in my tracks.

Hands grab my shoulders, stopping me from tumbling to the ground. Looking up, I realize it's Marcus in front of me and my heart stops. Gazing into those gorgeous blue eyes, I'm lost.

"We need to talk." Without waiting for my response, Marcus tugs on my arm. Pulling me down the hallway and shoving me into the restroom. He doesn't let go of me until we're standing in front of the stalls.

"Are you sure talking to me is a good idea?" My eyes hone in on him, following his movements as he attempts to wear a hole into the tiled flooring.

"Look, I'm sorry okay. I overreacted." Marcus stops in front of me. Laughter bubbles from between my lips.

"You overreacted?! You kissed me back." I almost shout at him. Voices outside the restroom are getting louder, closer. Grasping my arm, Marcus pulls me into one of the stalls and slams the door behind us, reaching around me and flipping the lock.

We're so close and I can feel the heat of his body seeping into mine. All I want to do is wrap my arms around him and pull him flush against me. To let him invade my personal space. But I don't move. The people the voices belong to enter the bathroom. Talking as, I can only assume, they make their way to the urinals.

"Are you going to Marcus' party at Franklin's on Saturday?" I don't recognize the voice and I open my mouth; Marcus places his finger over my lips shushing me.

This close to me all I can smell is him. What would he do if I sucked his finger into my mouth? Showed him just how skilled my tongue is? But I don't move, I don't speak. At this point, I don't even think I'm breathing.

"Sure, if he pushes Rachel away any further, I reckon I can sink my cock into that pussy again. I'm this close." The second voice is Jackson, my eyes snap to the door before I look back to Marcus. The other person laughs.

Marcus' face is impassive, I can't get a read him. Isn't he going to react to Jackson's comment? If that was my partner I'd be beating on Jackson's ass. My eyes scan over Marcus, but he doesn't move, just keeps his finger against my lips even though I don't plan on speaking.

"I wouldn't mind taking some sloppy seconds." They both laugh and I can hear the taps running as they wash their hands. When the door to the restroom shuts again, Marcus slowly removes his finger from my lips, tracing across my jawline and stroking the skin there.

"What the fuck?" I whisper, still not confident that Jackson and his friend won't hear me. Marcus takes a small step back, pulling his heat away from me. Raising a hand to his hair, he grabs on it, tugging slightly.

"Rachel and I...it's not working, it hasn't for a while." When I have seen Marcus these last few days he's always been with the guys, but the realization hits me that Rachel has never been with them.

"Then why not just end it?" my voice cracks, I want him to end it and be with me. But I don't think that is how this is going to go. He's already made it clear how he feels about me, about gay guys. Could I see him with another girl, or would it just drive me crazy?

"It's not that easy Trey, you wouldn't understand..." my eyes widen at his comment.

"What I wouldn't understand, being a gay guy, pretending to be straight? Of course not, cause that's not a situation I've ever been in. I've never been criticized or beaten up for my sexuality." My voice breaks as I speak, remembering the names my dad had called me. The punches I'd taken all because I was attracted to guys.

Marcus looks taken aback like he doesn't know what to say. My breath is coming out quick and sharp as I try and force down the memories but it's hard. My panic is rising, I'm not taking in enough oxygen, my body feels like it wants to shut down. My eyes close.

"Trey, are you okay?" the concern in his voice is obvious but he sounds so far away. Hands push against my shoulders, backing me into the stall's door holding me there. Images of my dad raising his fists to me flash before my closed eyelids.

Lips connect with mine; I inhale much-needed oxygen through my nose. A hand on my waist, and a hard body pushing against my own. Scrambling for purchase, my hands grab onto Marcus' jacket holding him against me. Our lips break apart and we're both left with our chests heaving.

"You're okay, I got you." Marcus' hand works its way under the hem of my t-shirt rubbing small circles against my skin. His touch is electrifying and pulls me away completely from those awful memories. His lips are still close to mine and we are breathing the same air.

CHAPTER TWENTY-SEVEN

Marcus

I kissed Trey and it just made everything feel right in the world. I fucked up originally, messed up what I was trying to say. But after days of avoiding him, I feel awkward around him. Whenever I'd seen him I always made sure I left the vicinity.

Not because I didn't want to see Trey, but because I couldn't trust myself around him. I have wanted so much to apologize to him for my harsh words; I saw the hurt on his face and it broke my heart every time I remembered.

After days of watching him sulk around the halls, his eyes downcast as I watched him from the shadows, unseen, had eventually forced me to seek him out. I wanted to tell him I was ending it with Rachel, that I wanted to be with him, but I needed time.

Since our confrontation in the restroom, and his ensuing panic attack, it had made up my mind. His body and lips melded so perfectly to mine, and I couldn't get enough of him. I was still avoiding Rachel and I knew she wasn't pleased but I was beyond caring. I just needed to bide my time for now.

It's now Saturday, my birthday, and I asked Trey to come to the party and he reluctantly agreed. We had brief moments together since I admitted to him that I needed time, lingering in the locker room after gym class and disappearing into the shadows, our lips always finding each others.

Our hands sometimes brushing in the hallways as I stuck to my friends, and he stayed with Nate. Our eyes connecting as we crossed paths.

Sitting now on Franklin's couch I'm waiting for my party to begin and the pizza he ordered to arrive. Heading into the kitchen, I grab a can of soda from the fridge. Opening it, I chug it down and throw the empty into the trash.

A hand trails across my ass and I flinch; Rachel circles around to the front of me. My eyes scan over her outfit, her tiny, pleated skirt barely covers her ass, and her breasts are almost spilling out of her top. God, she's beautiful, but the inside definitely doesn't match the outside.

Over the last few days I've really looked at myself, I'm not gay, that much I know. I'm still attracted to women but turns out, I'm attracted to guys too. That wasn't something I saw coming.

Rachel steps even closer to me, rubbing her body up against mine and purring in my ear. Her tongue flicks against the outside of it.

"God, I've missed you, Marcus. I've not seen you all week." Her hand rubs against my dick through my jeans, but there's no reaction. "Happy birthday baby, want to go upstairs so I can give you your present?"

Wrapping my fingers around hers, I pull her hand away from my crotch and step back, trying to get some distance from her.

"The party's about to begin, what kind of birthday boy would I be if I wasn't here when people arrive?" I let out a soft chuckle.

"But Marcus, I'm horny. I need you to fuck me." She thinks she sounds sultry but all it does is make me cringe. "You should feel how wet I am." Rachel goes to take another step toward me, and I step back again.

"I said no Rachel. Not right now!" The sound of the doorbell cuts her off before she can speak again, and I turn on my heel making my way to the front door.

After that it's a whirlwind of answering the door and welcoming people, even though it's Franklin's house and he arranged this, he said it's my birthday and has left me in charge of greeting people. Or more to the point, he and Chelsey disappeared a while ago and I haven't seen them since.

The next time the doorbell rings and I open it, Trey's standing there. He's wearing tight black jeans with rips in the knees, and his usual Converse. The sleeves are rolled up on his black shirt, and I can see the tattoos that adorn his lower arm. I finish looking him over, my tongue darting out over my dry lips.

"Marcus, happy birthday." Trey steps across the threshold, his hand brushing against mine.

"You made it." It's the happiest I've sounded all evening, thankfully there's no one else to hear it, the entryway is empty. "I could do with some help grabbing some...stuff from the basement. Give me a hand?"

"Lead the way," Trey smirks and throws me a wink. There isn't a single thing I need in the basement, but I need to get him alone. Leading the way, Trey follows behind me and we make our way down into the basement, not closing the door entirely but leaving it open enough that the light shines down some of the stairs.

Turning the light on at the bottom, I grab his hand and tug Trey with me till my back hits the wall. Dragging his lips to mine, I let them connect, thrusting my tongue straight into his mouth and tangling our tongues together. My hands are all over him, and his hands return the favor.

Gasping, I feel his hardening dick rubbing against my length, we swallow each other's moans. A small creak from the door has us pulling apart and we look over to the stairs.

"There's no one there, someone must have caught the door." I pull him back to me and we trade kisses for a few more minutes before we reluctantly pull apart.

"We should probably get back to the party, someone's gonna start missing you." Nodding, I kiss his lips one last time, both of us having to readjust our hard lengths.

We head for the stairs, but I stop Trey. Passing him a box of sodas as we pass, I grab another for myself before signaling with a nod to the stairs. It doesn't look like I've been missed when we exit into the hallway. Taking the boxes into the kitchen, we place them on the countertop.

"Marcus. Buddy. Where have you been?" Franklin shouts from the doorway, I point at the boxes. "Rachel said she needs to talk to you. She's in the spare room." Franklin grabs a can of soda before leaving Trey and I stood there.

"I better go see what she wants, hopefully, it's not my *birthday gift*," signaling quotations with my fingers, "she wanted to give me earlier." Trey rolls his eyes; he knows exactly what kind of birthday gift Rachel would want to give me.

Leaving him in the kitchen I head for the stairs, ascending them slowly wanting to give myself time to prepare for whatever Rachel is about to throw at me. Knowing my luck she's going to be naked in the spare room waiting for me to fuck her. But that's not going to be happening, not at all.

I reach the landing making my way to the bedroom, the door is slightly ajar. I knock gently but there's no response. The door opens a little more from my knuckles rasping against it. I can hear moans now, fuck. Maybe Franklin meant she was waiting in his room. I move my hand to the handle to close the door.

"Fuck Jackson, fuck me harder!" Rachel's voice is clear from inside the room. Without thinking, I push the door open.

Rachel is on her hands and knees on the bed, Jackson has his jeans around his ankles. His dick thrusting in and out of her pussy. I know he said he wanted to fuck her, but I didn't think he actually would. Not while we are supposed to be *together*. I thought our friendship meant more than that. I just stare, watching as Jackson fucks her harder.

Jackson runs his fingers around where they are joined, running them up to her ass. He pushes his finger into her, and she lets out a small scream, her head tilting in my direction, she smirks.

"What. The. Actual. Fuck!" I shout, finally finding my words. Jackson stops suddenly but Rachel continues pushing and pulling back and forth on his dick.

"Oh, don't stop on the account of Marcus, Jackson. He can have me next." Jackson blinks, but makes up his mind, resuming his thrusting.

"You fucking bitch! If you want him so much, why not just break up with me?" My fists are clenching at my sides, my anger rising. If she just ended this farce that is our supposed relationship it would be one less thing to deal with.

"Jealous...Marcus?" she speaks around her moans. "Maybe you...should have...gotten in first." Jackson's rhythm doesn't falter, his eyes are closed now, and I can see he's close. Rachel moans one last time, her own eyes fluttering closed as she comes. With a roar, Jackson rips his dick from her pussy, his cum spurting all over her back.

"Fuck you, Rachel. It's over." With no more words to say to her I turn and leave. Her shouts follow me as I exit the room, but I ignore anything she has to say.

Walking down the stairs, Trey is waiting for me at the bottom, his eyes take in my clenched fists, and the anger reflected in my eyes.

"It's done, it's over." Without another word, I walk straight out of the front door hoping that Trey will be behind me.

CHAPTER TWENTY-EIGHT

Trey

Walking across the street we head for the house I'd seen Marcus' Jeep parked outside the week before. Thinking Marcus will head inside, I'm shocked when he swerves toward his Jeep and jumps in. Scrambling to get inside I slam the door behind me. Marcus tears off the driveway.

"What just happened?" I position myself in the seat to look over at Marcus. His hands are gripping the steering wheel, his knuckles going white. Marcus' cell phone chimes in his pocket but he ignores it.

"Rachel was fucking Jackson... I saw everything." Marcus keeps flexing his hands, I want to reach out to him but he seems volatile. Will he go after Jackson?

"I'm so sorry." What else can I say?

"It's fine, I wanted to end it. She just made it easier for me." Marcus reaches over to the stereo and flicks it on. The music ending our conversation.

Sitting back in the seat, I look out the window. I have no idea where Marcus is taking us, but I just let him drive. Even in silence, I enjoy his company. Resting my hands on my jeans, I rub my hands across the fabric.

The more he drives, the more I can see the tension leaving his body, his posture relaxing bit by bit. I watch him, drinking in every detail about him. When we eventually stop, we're parked at a lookout. Marcus turns off the engine and gets out. Exiting the Jeep, I follow him.

"I come here when I need to think." Marcus doesn't turn to me, he just looks out over the small town below us.

Standing beside him, I want to touch him. Tentatively I reach my hand out, our fingers brushing. The small electrical jolt, I've felt before zaps up my arm. Marcus gasps. Does he feel it too? We lock our fingers and just stand there.

"So, what now?" Absentmindedly I stroke my thumb over Marcus', hoping my touch will soothe him completely. His cell phone rings again, and he takes it out of his pocket silencing it.

"I still need time Trey. I'm not ready to tell people about us." His head turns, his eyes drifting to my face. "My dad's not always a nice guy." I flinch slightly, all too familiar with dad issues. Marcus squeezes my hand. "I don't think he will react well, but I want this. I want us."

Pulling me closer, Marcus turns to face me, taking up my other hand. Our fingers interlock. He closes the gap between us, his lips brushing against mine. It feels so right to be here with him. I've never wanted someone so much in my life, and I hope Marcus feels the same way.

His hands drift up to the bare skin on my forearms making me shiver. Continuing their path up to my neck. Lips brush against the cheekbone on one side of my face, his hand cupping my other cheek. My hands rest gently on his hips, my fingers slipping through the belt loops and pulling his crotch in line with mine.

"Stay with me tonight. My parents aren't home." Marcus

whispers into my ear, his tongue flicks out, running up the outside of my ear and I moan. Nodding, I let him take me by the hand and walk me back to his Jeep. When we reach his Jeep, I expect him to open the door for me, but instead, he pushes me back against it.

Marcus cages me inside his arms, resting a hand on either side of my body. Our lips meet once more and our tongues tangle. Exploring each other's mouths, our crotches push against each other. We're both hard, as much as I'd love him to drop to his knees and wrap his mouth around my cock, this isn't what it's about right now.

Pushing back from me, Marcus looks into my eyes, his breath heaving. Without another word, he walks around the other side of the Jeep and gets in. Trying to catch my breath and calm my heart rate, I fumble for the door handle, when I get it open, I climb straight in.

The drive back to Marcus' seems so much shorter than on the way out here, and when we pull into the driveway, I'm out before the engine has even stopped. Looking over at Franklin's house, I realize the party is still going on.

Marcus stalks to the front door and opens it, waiting for me to enter before he closes and locks it behind me. The house is silent and all the lights are off. Without turning a single light on, Marcus makes his way to the stairs and I follow.

Walking me down the hallway he goes into a room on the left. Stepping across the threshold, it hits me how it's so Marcus in here. Posters adorn the walls, and there are a few trophies on the shelves along with some books. I look around taking in the entire room.

Marcus strips off his jacket and t-shirt, letting them drop to the floor. My mouth waters as my eyes track up and down his naked chest. A small spattering of hair leads down to the waistband of his jeans. Flicking the button on his jeans, he lowers the zip letting his jeans hang low on his narrow hips.

"Are you going to keep staring? Or are you going to get undressed?" My eyes snap to Marcus' and he smirks. That smirk is dangerous, his lips quirking up makes me want to lick him. To taste him again. My fingers fumble with the buttons on my shirt.

When I finally get them undone, I take off my shirt and lay it on the desk chair next to the door. Kicking off my Converse, I undo my jeans and let them drop to the floor pushing them to one side. My cock is hard, tenting my boxers. I look up to Marcus, his jeans are now gone. His own cock is straining against the fabric of his boxers.

Marcus moves toward me, his eyes looking up and down my body, he licks his lips. Taking my hand, he walks me to the edge of the bed and pushes me down. Once I'm sprawled back on the bed, he moves to the other side and lies down next to me.

I've screwed around a lot with guys since I realized I was gay, we've kissed, and engaged in heavy petting. Sucking each other off until release, but I've never just slept with another guy, in either sense of the word 'sleep'.

Throwing a leg over my hips, he pulls me against him. Our hands and our lips explore each other, but we never touch each other or our own cocks. Just letting our clothed lengths rub together, it's almost enough to make us both cum.

Our bodies are tangled around each other. We're both exhausted, Marcus' breath evens out and I finally let sleep claim me. A smile fixed on my lips.

CHAPTER TWENTY-NINE

Marcus

The days since breaking up with Rachel have been perfect, I've felt so much more relaxed than I ever have since we started dating. It's like a weight has been taken off my shoulders. I've had several calls and texts from her begging me to take her back. But I don't budge.

I'm happy where I am right now, waking up the morning after my birthday with Trey beside me. I didn't want to get out of bed. Preferring to stay in our own little world. But eventually, we had to get back to real life. Still hiding from other's eyes. We've gone a week in our new reality.

When I get home from the movies with Franklin the house is mostly silent, I can hear voices drifting from the dining room. Heading in that direction, I drop my keys on the side table before heading through the door. Stopping abruptly, I take in the scene before me.

My mom and dad are sitting at the table, but the person that surprises me is Rachel. My mom has Rachel's hand clasped in her own rubbing small circles on the back of Rachel's hand. Looking at Rachel, her mascara is streaked down her face like she's been crying.

"Eh...what's going on here?" My dad's eyes cut to my own.

"Rachel was just telling us you two had broken up, Marcus!" Anger laces his words, that man has always thought Rachel and I were perfect for each other. Appearances are the only thing that matter to him, not my happiness and Rachel fits that perfectly despite the reality of her vile personality. Rachel whimpers, my mom starts making cooing noises at her.

"Yeah, we aren't right for each other dad." I don't move from where I'm standing but I fold my arms across my chest. My dad stands suddenly, knocking the dining chair back with a thump.

"And who *is* right for you Marcus? Because Rachel has been telling us some interesting things!" His voice is calm, but his face is starting to glow bright red, like it does just before he explodes.

Slamming his hands on the table my mom and Rachel both jump. "She says you've been spending a lot of time with some guy called Trey. That she's seen you..." he stammers over his words, his face getting redder by the second "...kissing...". My heart plummets.

My face blanches as my eyes dart to Rachel's, with my mom and my dad's attention both on me she smirks at me. The look of malice on her face is incredible, she looks ready to destroy me.

"No...no...that's not the reason." My body shakes, how had she seen us, when had she seen us? I didn't wholly break up with her because of Trey, I'd broken up with her because she was cheating on me with Jackson, and god knows how many other guys. "Tell them the truth Rachel!"

As my parent's faces cut back to Rachel, she returns to the weak and pathetic act she's been displaying for them already. "I...I did Marcus...I can't believe you did that to me... I love you..." she starts crying again and my mom pulls her into her arms, gently rubbing her hand up and down her back. Rachel's body shakes from the intensity of the sobs coming from her mouth.

"I don't know what she's been telling you, but it's all lies!" I raise my voice. It's not all lies but I can't let them know that. My dad storms around the table grabbing me by the front of my t-shirt.

"I will have no son of mine sucking dick!" Spit flies from his mouth into my face. My hands scramble trying to get purchase on his arms as he shakes me violently. The vein in his forehead is bulging. It's been a long time since I've seen him this angry, and never in my direction.

Digging my fingers into his forearms I try and get him to release me, but his grip is like steel. Out of the corner of my eye, I see my mom pulling Rachel up and leading her toward the hallway. My mom's arm is wrapped around Rachel's shoulders. The look of venom Rachel throws me over her shoulder has me swallowing hard. This isn't the end of it.

"Listen to me boy!" My dad shakes me again, "You will go to that girl right now, beg her for forgiveness, and ask her to take you back!"

Shaking my head, "I can't do that dad..." my voice sounds weak, "You don't understand." I drop my arms to my sides, there is no way my dad is going to release me until he's good and ready to.

"I don't care how you feel about this Trey person, it's over!" Finally releasing me, I sag slightly taking in huge gulps of air. My body is still shaking.

"This is nothing to do with Trey, dad," I feel the courage I've been lacking since entering the dining room. "Rachel's been fucking around behind my back." All I hear is a roar a split second before my dad's fist connects with my face, not prepared for it, the hit knocks me to the floor. My dad looms over me.

"Don't you dare put the blame on Rachel! You've been cheating on her with that... boy", his fists are clenched at his sides as he says the word boy, "...and now you say she was the one cheating. You're pathetic!"

My dad starts to lean toward me, and I scramble backward trying to get away from him. My back collides with the wall and my dad advances on me. I can feel the blood dripping down my face. Grabbing me by my neck, he drags me up the wall, holding me against it.

"I swear boy, if I have to beat the gay out of you, I will!" The venom lacing his voice leaves me trembling. Lifting my arms up to try and protect my face, I wait for the next hit, but it doesn't come, instead, his grip on my neck tightens.

Trying to pull air in and finding I no longer can. I kick out with my feet but hit nothing but air. With the lack of oxygen and the hit to my face starting to take effect, I see black spots jumping across my vision. When I feel like I'm on the verge of passing out my dad lets go of my neck but continues pushing me against the wall. Looking up at him I see the satisfied look on his face.

"Maybe beating it out of you isn't the way. I could always beat it out of Trey, though if he's managed to get his claws into you, it might take a while."

With strength I shouldn't possess, I grab my dad by the front of his shirt and shove him back. Stumbling he catches himself on the dining table. "You. Won't. Touch. Him!" My voice is loud but hoarse. "You won't touch *me*!" Whirling on my feet, I start to walk away but my dad grabs my shoulder stopping me in my tracks.

"And who is going to stop me, Marcus? You?" his bark of laughter sends shivers down my spine. Pushing his hand from my shoulder, I step into the hallway and grab my bag and keys. I see movement ahead of me, my mom is leaning on the living room door shaking her head. She thinks this is all my fault. When my hand connects with the front door handle his voice booms, "If you walk out Marcus, don't come back!"

Ignoring the threat, I wrench open the door and it slams into the wall, I don't even bother to close it behind me as I jog over to my Jeep and climb inside and lock the doors. Reaching up, I wince as my fingers touch my throbbing and bleeding cheek.

Where am I going to go? My eyes look in the rearview mirror at Franklin's house. I'm sure he would let me stay with him, but if my dad comes looking for me, that's the first place he's going to go.

Pulling out of the drive, I decide I need to drive around a little, clear my head before I make any more rash decisions.

CHAPTER THIRTY

Trey

Lying back on my bed with a towel slung around my hips from my shower, and my eyes closed, my mind drifts to Marcus. We'd come a long way since that first day at school. What seemed like only yesterday was now a couple of weeks ago. What had started with stolen glances across the classroom, had become stolen kisses and private moments between the two of us.

Now he's broken up with that bitch Rachel for cheating on him with Jackson, on his birthday of all things, maybe we can move forward. I'll give him the time he's asked for though. A loud banging on the front door has me jolting upright. Who the fuck? Picking up my cell I check the time, it's 9:30 p.m. Mom isn't due home from work for a few more hours.

Scrambling off my bed, I drop my towel to the floor and grab some sweats. The banging sounds again as I make it to the hallway.

"Jesus, hang on, I'm coming," I mutter, racing down the stairs. Flinging the door open, my heart stops.

Standing on the porch is Marcus, his eyes downcast. Even

in the dark, I can see the black circle under one eye, and dark crusted red on his cheekbone. Inhaling sharply, I step through the doorway and stand in front of him. He doesn't even look up at me, his whole body shaking.

Without thinking, I grab his hands and pull him through the door, kicking it closed behind him. I don't utter a word as I reach forward, resting my fingers under his chin I slowly lift his head. With the light in the hallway, I can now see his face fully.

The dark circle under his eye is swollen and bruised. His cheek is split, and blood has dripped down it to his chin, long since dried now. Tracing my eyes over the rest of his face looking for more damage I see none, dropping my gaze down I notice the mottled bruising on his neck.

"Fuck!" My voice seems to startle him, and his haunted, empty blue eyes jump to my own. "What the fuck happened? Who did this to you?"

Shaking his head, "Rachel...she..." his words trail off. I clench my fists at her name.

"What the fuck did she do? I'll fucking end her!" my voice rising causes Marcus to flinch again. I can't stop the anger building within me.

"It wasn't her...well it was," his voice trembles as he talks, "I got home and...and she was with my mom and dad. They know." Those two words leave me devastated. How did she know? We'd been so careful, and the first thing she does is tell Marcus' parents.

Marcus has already explained to me that his dad would never accept his sexuality, just like my own hadn't. It's why we have always made sure no one saw us. Marcus had wanted to tell his parents, but not yet. Lacing my fingers with his, I begin leading him to the stairs, "Come on, we've got to get you cleaned up."

Following me up the stairs to my bedroom, I walk us

AGAINST THE
ODDS

S Lucas

inside and direct him to the bed. Marcus just stands there, the backs of his knees pressing against the edge of the bed, his eyes flitting around my room, and his whole body still trembling.

Dropping his hand from my own, I walk back to my bedroom door to close and lock it. When I turn back around, he still hasn't moved. As I edge closer to him, his eyes lift and fixate on my chest before snapping up to mine. Gently I push him down so he's sitting on my bed before disappearing into the bathroom to grab the first aid kit. Deja vu much, though this time the roles are reversed.

Squatting down on my haunches, I survey the damage to his skin again. If I ever get my hands on his dad, Marcus won't be the only one with cuts and bruises. And Rachel... that's a whole other story. That bitch is going down.

Removing an antiseptic wipe from the wrapper, I methodically start to wipe the encrusted blood away from his cheek, avoiding the cut the best I can. Although Marcus still flinches each time it comes in contact with his skin.

Once I've wiped all the dried blood away, I move to the cut, Marcus grasps my cover between his fists, gritting his teeth with each pass. "I'm sorry."

Marcus lets out a weak laugh, "I should suck it up, yours was so much worse." His eyes scan to the pink scar just above my eye. When his fingers come in contact with the skin there, a shudder racks my body.

"Well, you'll be happy to know, stitches aren't required." Giving him a slight smile, his fingers are still touching the scar. With speed I wasn't expecting, Marcus lurches forward. His lips smash into mine, his hand moving around the side of my head and gripping onto my hair, tugging me forward as he lies back on the bed.

Scrambling up, I fall onto the bed on top of him. My legs fall to either side of his thighs, and my arms to either side of his head. A gasp rushes past my lips, and he takes the opportunity to thrust his tongue between them. We shouldn't be doing this, not at this moment in time, but it feels so good.

Nipping at his lower lip causes a groan to escape him, his hands running down my back leaving a path of heat in their wake, even though his hands feel ice cold. Resting on one hand, I trail the other down his side till my fingers ghost the edge of his t-shirt, before disappearing under it.

When my hand comes in contact with his skin, I realize his hands aren't the only cold thing. Pulling back abruptly, I look down at Marcus, he's shaking and it's not from lust, but the chills that have taken over his whole body.

Jumping up and away from him, his dilated eyes track my movements. His breath is coming in short, sharp rasps and I can see his cock pushing against the front of his jeans. "We can't do this..." god I want nothing more than to do this but not right now.

"Wait...what!" Marcus sits up, confusion marring his features, his shoulders slumping.

"No, I don't mean at all, you're freezing Marcus. We need to get you warmed up." Grasping his arm, I tug Marcus up from the bed and drag him inside the bathroom, closing the door. Letting go, I walk over to the shower and turn the knobs until the water starts up. Running my fingers under the spray, I wait until it heats up.

Turning back to Marcus I move closer to his shaking form, lifting his t-shirt I pull it over his head and drop it to the floor. Locking my eyes with his, I drop to my knees before him and raise my hands to the waistband of his jeans. Flicking the button open, I pull the zipper down carefully over his hard cock causing him to inhale sharply.

Marcus toes off his sneakers, kicking them to the side as I tug down his jeans and boxers, when they reach his feet, he rests a hand on the counter and steps out of them. Just in his socks, his cock stands proudly before me, but I refuse to take my eyes from his.

Standing back up, I don't once take my eyes from Marcus even when he reaches down to remove his socks. His shaking has lessened but it's probably down to the fact the steam from the shower is warming up the room.

"Get in the shower Marcus."

CHAPTER THIRTY-ONE

Marcus

At the sound of Trey's voice telling me to get in the shower, I step forward under the spray. Compared to my freezing body, the warm water feels like hundreds of tiny shards stabbing into my skin. Flinching, I grit my teeth and push on until I'm entirely under the shower head, the water catching my abused skin has me grinding my teeth even harder.

Hearing the shower door close behind me, I think Trey has left me on my own until I feel the heat of his naked body against my back. His arms wrap around my waist, and his hands clasp in front of my abs.

"I got you," his voice is soft, barely a whisper next to my ear. My shoulders slump, the events of the evening leaving me emotionally and physically drained.

When I'd left my house, I'd driven around for a while, before finally heading up to the lookout point, and sitting on the hood of my Jeep. All I could think about was the anger on my dad's face, my mom shaking her head at me in disappointment, and the glint in Rachel's eyes as she wrapped my parents up in her sob story.

Part of it had been true, Trey and I had shared the odd stolen kiss here and there, but how did she even know that? The real reason I'd ended it was because of seeing her and Jackson fucking. Before Trey, I could have pushed past her shoving her tongue down his throat, while he finger fucked her at the movies.

But seeing her moaning like some two-bit hooker as Jackson thrust into her pussy from behind, had pushed me over the edge. I probably should have ripped Jackson from her and beat the life out of him. That's probably what she wanted, instead, I'd told her it was over and simply walked away.

Pulling myself out of my thoughts, I concentrate on the feel of Trey's body wrapped around mine, his arms tightly banded around me, and his dick nestled against my ass cheeks. Resting his chin on my shoulder, he peppers soft kisses along the side of my neck, a quiet moan escaping my lips.

I can feel my body slowly accepting the heat from not just the water but his body too, the water no longer feels like it's stabbing me all over and my muscles start to relax. Turning inside the cage of Trey's arms, I look into his sparkling green eyes, a small smile tugging on my lips before it disappears.

"I have nowhere to go..." the realization suddenly hits me, but Trey's arms only tighten around me, his fingers rubbing small circles into my lower back.

The frown on his face shows his confusion. "What do you mean? You're staying here."

"I'll sleep on the couch. It'll only be for a few days till I work out what I'm doing."

"You can stay here as long as you need Marcus, I don't want you going back to that house, back to your dad. My mom won't mind."

Trey's arms finally leave me, and he grabs the shower gel.

Soaping up his hands, he reaches for mine. When our fingers connect, I feel a now familiar tingle racing up my arms. Slowly and methodically, Trey starts to wash my exhausted body.

Trailing his hands up my arms until he reaches my bruised neck, I can't help the tiny flinch as his fingers connect with the damaged tissue. Leaning his face toward mine, he captures my lips in the softest kiss I've ever felt.

He doesn't demand entry, just presses his lips against my own while he washes my neck. When he's finished, his lips disappear, and his hands make their way across my chest and abs. He massages the muscles as he goes, my cock jerking at every touch. Reaching lower and lower, he stops at the v where my waist tapers off.

Grasping my length all of a sudden in his fist, I inhale sharply. His touch is like nothing I've ever felt before, it feels so different from that moment in Franklin's bathroom. But he isn't trying to get me off this time, his sole purpose right now is to take care of me. Has anyone ever cared for me like this before? I can't think of a single person.

Once he has deemed me clean there, he slowly kneels in front of me, peppering brief kisses to my chest and abs before he finally comes to a stop on his knees. His face now level with my dick, it would be so easy for him to part his lips and suck me down.

Reaching for his head I run my fingers through his hair, hoping he will understand what I want him to do. Instead of taking me in his mouth, he runs his lips gently up and down the sides of my rock-hard length while cleaning my legs.

The frustration building inside me is a welcomed difference to the hurt and anger caused by Rachel and my family. I want nothing more than for Trey to make me come with his mouth, or his hands. I don't care at this point; I just need the release.

CHAPTER THIRTY-TWO

Trey

When I stand, my eyes connect with Marcus'. His pupils are blown with the smallest ring of blue around the black. His breath coming out in pants. I watch as the soap suds run down his body, and over his rigid cock. Shutting off the water, I grab two towels from the rack, wrapping one around my waist.

Turning back to Marcus, I smirk when I notice he's been looking at my ass. Trying to get rid of my dirty thoughts I struggle to concentrate on the fact I need to comfort him, not thinking of all the ways I can get him off.

Swallowing hard, I beckon Marcus to me with a simple hand gesture. When he steps from the shower, I wrap the towel low on his waist, his erection still evident. Tracing my fingers down his arm, I lace my fingers with his and squeeze before turning and directing him back into my bedroom.

Leading him to my bed I let go of his hand and turn my back on him, trying to get my breathing under control. I've been with guys before, but I've never wanted to take it any further. Well, that was until that first kiss with Marcus.

Opening my drawers, I grab out two pairs of shorts and

turn back to Marcus. The towel I gave him is now dropped on the bed behind him, and his hand is fisted around his cock. Moving up and down it rhythmically, he looks up to my eyes.

"Fuck Trey, I need you," Marcus' voice is barely a whisper, but it breaks something inside me. Dropping the shorts to the floor leaving them forgotten, I'm in front of him in a flash. Pushing him back onto the bed, I crawl up the mattress beside him.

Flinging my legs on either side of him I straddle his thighs, his length pushing against my ass cheeks through the towel still slung around my hips. Reaching down I feather my fingers across his chest, moving down toward his navel and back up again.

When the tips come in contact with Marcus' nipples his breathing stutters. Looking up to his face I find his eyes closed, his lips parted.

Moving back along his body, my towel rubs against his erection causing his hips to jerk and his breath to hitch. Leaning forward on one arm, I blow lightly across one nipple before moving over to the other, his whole body shuddering.

Darting out my tongue, I trace the outline of his hardening nipple before wrapping my lips around the protrusion. Marcus' hand grasps onto my hair, tugging at it slightly, holding my mouth to his chest. Flicking my tongue over the hardened bud has Marcus' cock jerking again, smacking against my stomach.

My own stiff length pushes against my towel, making me groan against his nipple as my piercing brushes against the soft fabric sending shivers down my spine. With his hand slipping from my hair, Marcus trails his fingers down my back until he reaches the edge of the towel.

With a yank Marcus pulls the towel from around my waist, our cocks connect, making us both moan. I can't help it as my hips push forward rubbing our lengths together. Crawling my way back up Marcus, I brush my lips up his chest until our lips connect.

Our bodies rub against each other in all the right places, heat traveling from my head to my toes. Brushing my hand down Marcus' side, I reach between us, grasping both of our cocks together. Our moans mingle as our lips clash together, the ring at my tip brushing against Marcus' sensitive head.

Releasing my own cock, I fist Marcus'. My hand makes short, sharp motions up and down his steely length. Marcus pants against my lips, our tongues dueling as they fight for dominance. Biting down on my lower lip and running his tongue over the metal ring through it, Marcus drags another moan from me.

My hand jerking around his length speeds up, the frustration we're both feeling leaching from our bodies. Yanking his teeth away from my lip, Marcus tilts his head back. His eyes are closed, with his fists clutching at my bedsheets, a loud groan rips from his mouth as he finally cums.

His seed splatters across his abs and stomach. "Holy shit!" His voice is hoarse and he's panting again. I kiss his lips softly one last time, my body hovering over his as I shuffle myself back down once more. My tongue trailing over his chest as spasms from his release still rack through him.

Settling myself between his open legs and reaching his abs, I run my tongue from his groin to his belly button, lapping up his cum as I go. Wrapping my fingers around my still hard shaft I jerk myself closer, and closer to my own release.

It abruptly hits me as I lick up the last of the mess on Marcus' stomach. My balls tighten, almost on the verge of pain. Roaring I cum onto Marcus' discarded towel. Dropping my head down, my cheek rests against Marcus' hip, my breath fanning out over his heated skin.

Our bodies are both still trembling, I close my eyes trying to steady my breathing. Coming down slowly from the epic high I just hit. I nearly jump out of my skin when Marcus rests his hand on my cheek, I reach my own hand up to his and lace our fingers once more, giving his hand a squeeze that he returns.

When my breathing is steady again, I push myself up and off the bed, looking down at Marcus. His eyes are closed, and his breathing is almost back to normal. Grabbing the now cum stained towel from the end of my bed, I launch it into the laundry and move to grab the forgotten shorts from earlier.

Pulling them on I make my way back over to Marcus, his eyes opening when he hears my approach. I can see the tiredness in his eyes when I pass him the shorts. Saying nothing he stands before dragging them up his legs, covering his now flaccid shaft.

Throwing the other towel off the bed, I tug down the edge of the sheets pressing Marcus back until he sits back down. As soon as his ass hits the bed, he flops onto his side taking the sheet with him, his head connecting with the pillow. Making my way to the other side of the bed, I click off the light and crawl under the sheets.

Lying on my side facing Marcus. I wait for the tell-tale sounds of his breath evening out as he succumbs to sleep. When it comes, I feel like I can fully relax, and close my eyes.

CHAPTER THIRTY-THREE

Marcus

My eyes flutter open as I stretch out my stiff limbs. Staring at the ceiling, I realize I'm not in my own room. Sitting up suddenly, I look around, definitely not my room. The events of the previous day come flooding back.

Rachel sat with my parents, my dad with his hand wrapped around my throat as he held me against the wall, and then Trey as he wrapped his body around me in the shower. The pleasure he'd given me was indescribable.

The sound of vibrating catches my attention, my eyes snapping to the unit beside the bed where my cell phone lay. Grabbing for it I see I have ten missed calls from Franklin and a couple of texts. *Dude where are you? Rachel's been here causing shit.* Of course, she had! What had she told Franklin?

Don't worry, I'm safe is all I respond with before placing my cell back on the drawers. Dragging myself out of the bed I notice a t-shirt laid out for me. Grabbing it, I throw it on and make my way to the bathroom.

Looking in the mirror, I see the damage my dad had done to me the day before. Under my eye is swollen and bruised, there's the clear print of a hand on my neck. God, I look like shit, how am I even going to explain this to people.

They knew my dad was a hard ass, but he'd not raised his hand to me in years. A typical retired military man, my father lived for rules and they must be followed to the letter or face the consequences. Would anyone even believe me if I told them he'd done this?

Exiting the bathroom, I make my way to the closed bedroom door, opening it quietly, I stop and listen. I can hear voices drifting up the stairs. One is Trey, the other must be his mom. Leaving the bedroom, I walk barefoot down the stairs, my feet carrying me in the direction of the voices.

Entering the kitchen my eyes fall on Trey straight away, he's sat at the breakfast counter drinking a glass of orange juice. His mom is standing at the stove with her back to me. Her black hair tied in a messy bun on her head.

As she turns with the pan in her hand, she startles at my presence. Trey turns, his eyes honing in on me, the glass pressed to his lips. The same lips that were all over my body last night. My dick twitches slightly at the memories.

"Marcus…" Trey's voice is barely a whisper. Clearing his throat, he looks back to his mom, "Mom, this is Marcus. Like I said he's going to be staying here a few days."

Trey's mom's eyes look over my face studying me, her eyes stopping when she sees the bruising. Her sudden inhale of breath leaves me feeling nervous.

"Stay as long as you need to sweetie." Dropping her gaze from my face she starts dishing the eggs from the pan onto two plates alongside some bacon. When she turns her back on me, I look over to Trey again. Standing, he moves toward me before grabbing my hand, leading me to the stool next to his.

When I sit down Trey moves his own stool closer, pressing our thighs together. I can feel the heat from his body bleeding through his shorts. Placing his hand on my knee and squeezing, I flinch. My eyes flit to him, before moving to his mom, worried about what she will say if she sees us.

Trey lets go of my knee, grabbing the plates of food and placing them in front of us before filling an empty glass with orange juice and pushing it my way. Picking up a slice of bacon I shove it in my mouth, god I'm so hungry. I can't even remember when I last ate.

"I'm going to leave you boys to it, I have some errands to run in town." Walking to Trey she gives him a brief kiss on his cheek, making him blush slightly. As she reaches me, she places her hand on my shoulder. "You're always welcome here, Marcus." Patting my shoulder, she turns and she walks out.

Her words leave me stunned; she doesn't even know me but has said I can stay as long as I need to. I spotted the look of sympathy in her eyes as she patted my shoulder. Has Trey told her what happened?

"Hey, where did you go?" Trey's voice cuts me out of my thoughts.

"I was just thinking, I know your mom said I can stay but I don't want to impose." I think back to my dad's words, how he said he'd hurt Trey if I didn't walk away but I won't let him. After last night, I'm not sure if I can walk away. I'm falling for Trey Banks, and I'm falling hard.

"You'd never be imposing Marcus. I want you here." Forgetting about the food in front of me I turn to face Trey, pulling him around on his stool. With no words spoken, I lean toward him. My lips brushing against his before running my tongue along the seam. I can taste the saltiness of the bacon he's been eating.

Tugging him closer, I slip from the stool and stand between Trey's open legs. My fingers tracking up the sides of his neck making him shiver. Trey's hand reaches for the growing bulge in my shorts, but I smack his hands away.

Breaking our kiss, I pull back, "Not this time." Trey looks confused at my comment, but his eyes soon roll back when I push my hand inside his shorts grabbing onto his rock-hard length. The gasp that escapes his lips makes my own dick harder.

Shuffling to the edge of his stool Trey pushes his shorts down, his dick springing free to give me better access. I drop to my knees in front of him, not stopping the movement of my hand on his dick. "I've never done this before." My husky voice shocks me, but his soft moans spurn me on. "I want to taste you."

Leaning forward, I flatten my tongue and run it from the base of his dick all the way up the shaft, till I reach the piercing. The metal feels hot and hard against my tongue, swirling my tongue around it, Trey shudders. His hands are suddenly in my hair, tugging on the strands.

Keeping one hand at the base of his shaft working him up and down, I move the other to his balls squeezing them gently. Running my tongue around the head of his dick, stopping at his piercing each time to flick my tongue over it. I lick the pre-cum from his slit, he tastes incredible.

"Fuck, Marcus," tightening his hold on my hair, I expect Trey to push my mouth onto his dick, but he doesn't. Not wanting to disappoint though I open my mouth wide, taking him in. As soon as my mouth envelopes him, his hips jolt forward almost knocking him from the stool.

I can't help the laugh that escapes me, with my mouth around his dick the vibrations make him moan even more. Moving my mouth up and down, I hollow my cheeks trying to take more of him in. When his piercing hits the back of my throat I nearly gag, but his encouraging moans have me doing it again.

"Marcus, you need to stop, I'm going to cum." Ignoring his words, I work on him harder, my hand still rolling his balls between my fingers. The grip he has on my hair tightens further and I think he's going to pull me back instead he uses his fingers to guide me faster up and down his shaft.

With a couple of thrusts of his hips and a roar, Trey explodes his release, his load spurting down my throat, and I drink him down not wanting to waste a single drop. Using my tongue, I lick him clean, his body still quaking with aftershocks of his orgasm.

CHAPTER THIRTY-FOUR

Trey

Marcus moves back up my body tucking my softening cock back into my shorts. I can feel his own hard on brush against my inner thigh. His lips connect with mine and I can taste myself on him, but I couldn't care less. His kisses scorch me, making me feel more alive than I ever have, almost like a branding on my very soul.

Reaching behind his neck I lock my hands there, keeping his lips against my own. When banging comes from the front door, he jumps back abruptly. I feel bereft without him touching me. His eyes look toward the front of the house, his entire body suddenly stiffening up.

"What if it's..." I can see the terror in his eyes, he's wondering if somehow his dad found out he was here.

"If it's him, I'll send him packing!" Raising from the stool I make my way to the front door opening it, but it isn't Marcus' dad. Standing before me is Nate, his backpack slung over his shoulder. "Shit, sorry I forgot you were coming." Brushing my hand through my hair I realize I must look a state. My lips feel swollen from Marcus' kisses, and my cheeks are probably flush.

Stepping back from the door I motion for him to come inside. Once he's through the door, I close it behind him.

"Before we go any further, I need to let you know I have company." Nate's eyes dart to the living room door, his eyebrow raising.

"Oh, did someone get all hot and horny last night?" The laughter that comes from Nate makes me smile, it wasn't just last night.

"You could say that." Moving through the living room with Nate close on my heels we head for the kitchen.

"So, do I get to meet the mystery man?" Suddenly I feel nervous, Nate knows Marcus was dating Rachel and probably any of the other girls before her. What's he going to say when he realizes it's him? Maybe I should have told him to leave and come back later.

"Trey..." Marcus' voice calls from within the kitchen. Nate stops suddenly, grabbing my arm.

"Wait, is that Marcus Brady?" Shrugging his hand off me, I walk into the kitchen. Marcus has grabbed his seat back at the counter, but his eyes are fixed on the door. When Nate walks in behind me Marcus' eyes widen and he visibly swallows.

"So, are you two a thing now?" Nate walks to the fridge to get himself a soda.

"Yes"

"No" Marcus sputters at the exact same moment as I do. Nate shuts the fridge, his eyes playing tennis between Marcus and me. My mouth drops as I swivel to look at Marcus. "I mean, I don't know what this is."

Nate rounds behind Marcus resting his hand on his shoulder, "Don't worry dude, you got time to figure it out." Gesturing out before him "The weekend is still young."

Dropping into the seat next to Marcus, Nate starts geeking out about a new game he's just bought. Marcus doesn't even look like he knows how to answer, his life revolves around football, so video games don't seem like his thing.

Leaving them to their conversation I start cleaning up the plates from breakfast, my eyes every so often glancing over to my friend who is talking animatedly with his hands more than words, I can't help it when my gaze drifts to Marcus again. When he sees me looking, he offers me a small smile, his eyes lighting up.

Even with the damage to his face, he's still gorgeous. I can see what that bitch Rachel saw in him, he's one of the hottest guys I've ever seen. He's been an obsession since the first time I saw him in algebra during my first day.

I've been drawn to him ever since, like a moth to a flame and it's been dragging me closer ever since. After that first kiss at Franklin's pool party, I couldn't get enough of him even when he called me a queer and stormed out, leaving me there frustrated.

Watching two of the people I care about the most interacting, laughing, and joking makes me forget about all the shit in my past. I'll do anything to protect Marcus, even if it means taking on Rachel Turner, and his father.

CHAPTER THIRTY-FIVE

Marcus

Turns out I probably should have spent more time getting to know Nate, he may have been a geek, and definitely not into football or any kind of sports for that matter, but the guy is hilarious. He and Trey were meant to work on a project together but instead, we'd decided to watch movies.

Nate kept doing impressions of various characters which had my sides splitting with laughter. Trey and I had ended up starting a fight with the popcorn and when his mom had gotten home she just laughed at us and told us to make sure we cleaned up after ourselves.

Things at Trey's house were so relaxed, his mom didn't care when she caught us staring at each other, hands, on occasion, wandering further than they should. Nate didn't care either, he kept telling us how cute we were together. It was so easy to be around Trey, his mom, and Nate, I'd never felt so relaxed before.

When evening came and Nate headed home, Trey's mom cooked us all a late dinner which was beyond delicious, and I ended up going back for a second helping. She asked me about school and sounded interested in my life.

The topic turned to my family and I went quiet, but Trey had taken my hand in his and explained to her that my dad was the reason I was now staying at their home. His mom just nodded, accepting but asking for no further explanation.

After we finish dinner, Trey's mom says she is going to head to bed as she has the early shift at work in the morning. Trey and I start to clear away the dishes we used. Turns out even doing the simple task of washing and drying dishes, we can't keep our hands off each other.

Our hands keep brushing, sending shivers through me. And when Trey reaches past me to put the glasses away, I can't resist any longer. Turning in his arms I pull his lips to my own, the gasp that comes from his mouth gives me full access.

Sweeping my tongue across his, Trey pushes me back against the counter, his semi-hard dick pushing against my own. Every touch of his hands across my skin leaves heat in its wake. Trey is different from anyone else I've been with. For us, simple touches and kisses make me hard, leaving me panting.

Trey grabs my hand and pulls me from the kitchen back into the living room before he pushes me down on the couch. His heated gaze falls on my tented shorts and he licks his lips. Kneeling before me, he pulls at the waistband until I lift my ass so he can pull them down my legs.

My rock-hard dick stands to attention as Trey moves between my open legs, settling between my thighs. His lips capture my own and his fingers wrap around my dick. Moving, oh so slowly, up and down my shaft.

His tongue tangles with mine and I can't stop the small moan that escapes me as he works my dick up and down. Breaking away Trey leans back, a look of mischief in his eyes.

Scooting back ever so slightly, he moves his head down to my throbbing dick.

When his mouth envelopes me I nearly come right there and then, biting into my lip to stop the groan trying to escape. I don't want to wake his mom and have her coming downstairs and seeing us in such a compromising position.

Trey swirls his tongue around my hyper-sensitive head, his lip ring adding to the sensations running through me. I've imagined having his mouth around me but it's nothing compared to the actual reality of it.

Trey keeps the up and down motion on my dick with his mouth, his hands moving up the inside of my thighs, sending shivers down my spine.

Taking my balls in one hand, he rolls them between his fingers, and I can feel them tightening but I don't want to come yet. I don't want the feeling of his mouth on me to end but I'm not sure how much longer I can hold out for.

Popping my dick from his mouth Trey looks up at me and smiles, taking my dick in his hand once more, while the other releases my balls. Trey moves his empty hand to my face cupping my cheek and I turn to kiss the palm, his thumbs ghosting across my lips.

Darting out my tongue I lick the tip of his thumb, surprising even myself when I suck the digit into my mouth. Swirling my tongue around it like I would his dick. My eyes lock on Trey's and they are glazed, I can only presume mine are the same.

As I suck on his thumb Trey lets out his own moan, his hand gripping my dick but his motions having now slowed.

"I want to try something. But tell me to stop if it hurts." I can only nod as Trey grabs behind my knees and pulls me further down the couch till my ass is almost off the edge. He pulls his wet thumb from my mouth with an audible pop.

Moving back down to my dick, he licks around my balls

before licking from base to tip. His mouth descends over my hard length once more. He moves his hand between my legs ghosting his fingertips down my balls toward my ass.

Working his mouth up and down my dick faster he pushes his lubricated thumb against my anus. I can't stop my moans anymore, throwing my arm over my mouth I try to contain the sound. When the digit pushes past the tight ring of muscle, I groan.

Grabbing onto Trey's hair with my other hand, I push his head further down my dick and he takes every inch. The mixed sensations of Trey's mouth on my dick and his thumb moving in and out of my ass is game over. My balls tighten and I thrust my hips up as I push his mouth down.

My cum fills his mouth and I bite down on my forearm to disrupt my roar of pleasure. When I finally stop cumming, I'm panting. With one last lick, Trey releases me from his mouth, removing his thumb at the same time.

"Fuck, that was hot." Trey smiles up at me, "Come on quarterback we need some sleep." Before I have a chance to protest the fact he hasn't cum yet, he drags me to my feet and up the stairs to his bedroom.

CHAPTER THIRTY-SIX

Trey

My mom went to work early leaving Marcus and I with the house to ourselves. Jumping in the shower while Marcus is still in bed, I thought back over what had happened in the last day. Humming to myself I jump when Marcus wraps his arms around me.

We spend the day exploring each other's bodies, finding out what each of us likes. When we were both finally sated, we ended up in the shower again, washing each other which turned into another round of blow jobs.

Leaving the house, we jump in Marcus' Jeep heading for the diner, my mom had left a note and some cash telling us to go on a 'date' and enjoy ourselves, her treat. Pulling up outside Marcus looks across at me, his smile tight.

"I don't know if this is a good idea." Reaching across, I squeeze his hand.

"What, two friends can't grab dinner at the only diner in town?" Sure, I want people to know about Marcus and I, but only when he's ready for them to know. If that means a couple of hours not being able to touch him, then so be it.

Giving my hand a squeeze in return the smile on Marcus'

face becomes the real smile I've been seeing him give me all day.

"Okay, let's go!" Pushing open our doors we exit the Jeep and head inside the diner, grabbing a booth near the back.

Betsy comes over and takes both our orders, Marcus introduces us properly before she spins on her heel and heads to put our order in. Talking about school and football, we fill the time while we wait for our food to arrive.

Two plates of burgers and fries are dropped in front of each of us along with our sodas. Grabbing my glass, I take a sip, looking at Marcus across the table. The heat in his eyes is turning me on again, maybe not touching him for a few hours is going to be harder than I thought.

"Back to reality tomorrow then, school I mean." Marcus shrugs at me before grabbing a few fries from his plate. He's definitely nervous being here with me, but no one knows about us. Not yet anyway.

My gaze falters when I see Rachel walking into the diner with a few of the other cheerleaders over his shoulder. They head to the counter, but Rachel keeps looking our way, then to her phone. Shaking my head, I return my attention to my food and Marcus.

"I'm just going to go to the restroom." Marcus nods as he picks up his burger taking a bite. Standing I wipe my hands on the napkin and make my way to the back of the diner. I can see the emergency exit door swinging open, but figure they leave it open to take trash out.

The men's restroom door is just before the emergency exit and I turn and walk inside. I'm barely through when I'm hit across the back of the head. The force of the blow taking me to my knees. An arm yanks the back of my head and tightens around my throat. It cuts off my airway, and arms latch onto me dragging me to my feet.

I'm manhandled out of the restroom and out through the

emergency exit into the darkness outside and pulled into the side alley. Roughly I'm thrown to the ground, landing on my hands and knees, the gravel digging into my palms.

Confusion fills me, what the hell is going on? Before I can push myself to my knees a blow to my side takes me down to the ground entirely.

"Fucking homo! Thinking you can try it on with one of our friends!" I know that voice but before I can say his name, I get another kick to the side.

"I bet he wants to stick that gay dick of his right in Marcus' ass." A punch lands on my cheek.

"It's probably what he jerks himself off too, fucking faggot!" Another kick to my side.

"Let me guess, he turned you down and that's why you attacked him!" A fist connects with my forehead. Pulling my arms up I try to cover my head, curling into the fetal position.

The kicks and punches all over my body continue, and I try my best to protect myself. The words coming out of their mouths are vile, and so far from the truth. I care for Marcus and he cares for me.

I've heard all the names they call me before, my own father used them on me. You'd think after him, I'd have grown thicker skin, but they still hurt. They still aren't right.

I try to pull myself away from the pain, I imagine the way Marcus looks at me, his cheeks flushed, and his eyes glazed, even just after kissing. The feel of his hands on my body setting me on fire from head to toe.

With one more kick, this time to the head, everything goes black.

CHAPTER THIRTY-SEVEN

Marcus

I watch Trey's ass as he heads for the restroom, my view obscured as someone walks in front of it and sits down in the booth opposite me. Moving my gaze to who has sat across from me, my jaw almost hits the floor. Rachel. What the fuck does she want now.

"Looking good Marcus, considering." She grabs a French fry from Trey's plate, dipping it in ketchup before eating it. Her eyes staying on me the entire time.

"What do you want Rachel? Don't you think you've done enough?" My fists clench under the table. At this point she brings me nothing but revulsion, just being in her presence sets me on edge.

"I want what I've always wanted Marcus, you." She taps her manicured nails on the table. The sound going through me.

"But you can't have me anymore Rach, it's over." I'm trying so hard to not let her words affect me.

"It's over when I say it's over Marcus, haven't you realized that by now?" Running her foot up the side of my leg, I bite my lip trying not to scream at her to get off.

"You can't have me." Her foot is running higher up my leg toward my crotch. I slam my hand on the table making her jump but she carries on.

"I bet that I can Marcus, I mean I could always tell everyone at school all about you and Trey." Realizing she's taken her shoe off she pushes the underside of her foot against my soft dick. "That's where you've been since Friday isn't it, I know you haven't been at Franklin's."

"And what if I have? People at school aren't going to care. You've got nothing." The scowl on her face when I don't react to her foot rubbing against me disappears when she smirks.

"Don't I?" The twinkle in her eyes is terrifying. Reaching into her pocket she pulls out her phone. After scrolling down the screen, she turns the phone to me. My eyes widen, there on the screen is a picture of me and Trey kissing in Franklin's basement. His hands fisted in my shirt, and mine threaded through his hair.

Trey and I had thought we'd heard something, but we brushed it off, too consumed by each other to think of the possibilities.

As I reach for the phone, she pulls it back. The cackle that comes from her sends a chill down my spine.

"Tomorrow at school we're going to be back together, and you are never going to talk to Trey again. If I so much as see you looking his way, this picture will end up everywhere."

The food I've eaten is threatening to make a reappearance. I can feel the bile rising, and I swallow hard. My fists clench again.

"But for now, I think I've kept you here long enough, maybe we should go catch up with Jackson and Trey. I just want to make sure my point is made." Standing suddenly, she scoots out of the booth and holds her hand out to me. I ignore it and stand throwing what we owe for the food on the table.

Twirling she turns and heads in the same direction Trey had taken toward the restrooms, I follow close behind. She walks straight past the restroom doors and pushes through the emergency exit at the back of the diner.

When we get outside, I can hear the thumps and groans. Pushing Rachel out of the way I round the corner into the alley. There on the floor is Trey, he's covering his head with his hands, while Jackson and some of the other jocks kick him.

Charging forward, Jackson turns on me and grabs my shoulders pushing me back.

"Don't worry man, this faggot won't be coming onto you again. We dealt with him. Gave him a few bruises to match what he did to you." Arms wrap around me from behind, as I struggle against Jackson.

"I think that's enough now boys. I'm sure Trey here has learned not to come after my man again. Thank you again, Jackson." Her voice is overly sweet, and the words I want to say won't leave my throat.

"Don't worry sweetie, if he comes back again, I'm sure Jackson and the boys won't mind going another round." Jackson nods eagerly. Moving around me, Rachel gives me that sickly sweet smile. She leans closer to my ear, "In fact, if you go near him, next time I won't get them to stop."

The fight inside me drains away as I stare down at Trey's prone form. I want so much to reach out to him, to check he's okay but I know Rachel will sic her dogs on him again. There's no way I can take them all on. They'd kill him before I could stop them.

Reaching down for my hand, Rachel laces her fingers with mine. and I try not to shudder at her touch. "Come on lover, we got some catching up to do." Tugging at my hand Rachel pulls me down the alley, flanked on either side by Jackson and the other jocks.

When we reach the end of the alley, Rachel heads straight for my Jeep and leans up on the side of it. I fumble for my keys, taking my phone out of my pocket at the same time. As I round to my side, I send a quick text to Nate, thankful he gave me his number. *Trey. Alley behind the diner. Tell him I'm sorry.*

Getting into the Jeep, Rachel climbs in next to me. "Now take me home Marcus, there are lots of things I want to do to that body of yours, I'll make you forget him." With one last look at the alley, I start the engine and drive away.

CHAPTER THIRTY-EIGHT

Trey

Startling, I come back to consciousness, my whole body aching. I feel like one giant bruise, no inch of my skin unharmed. My eyes flutter open, and I can't help the groan that escapes my lips. Trying to focus on what I can see in front of me, I realize I'm sitting in someone's car.

"Trey...Trey can you hear?" Nate's voice sounds from beside me. Another groan from my parted lips. "Look, I'm taking you to the ER."

"Marcus..." my voice is hoarse, the pain in my neck throbbing.

"He's gone, Trey. He wasn't there when I found you," Nate's words rush out. "He sent me a text, told me where you were. He said he's sorry. This is so fucked up." Nate continues to mutter to himself. Shifting my body, the pain in my ribs intensifies.

I shuffle around so I'm facing Nate. He looks at me from the corner of his eye, he looks scared. Shit, I must look as bad I'm feeling, and if that's true, then I probably look like hell. Reaching out my hand, I rest it on his arm, and he jumps.

"No hospitals..." my hand flops back down between us.

"Trey, we have to go. You could have broken bones...what if one of your ribs punctured your lung...what if you die!" Nate's voice gets louder, almost high pitched as he speaks.

"Had worse," my mind drifts to the beatings my dad gave me once I came out. I think he was hoping his fists could take the gay away, but that never happened. He always made sure to hit me where it couldn't be seen, told me if I told anyone he'd go after my mom instead, so I kept quiet.

It wasn't until I walked out of the shower one day and found my mom in my room with a basket of laundry, that she saw the bruises. The yellow and purple fist marks adorning my skin. She'd gasped in horror and dragged me into her arms. She knew of the verbal abuse, but not the physical.

While holding me, she told me about the job she'd been offered in this small town, how she'd been wanting to get away from my dad since he'd turned on me. But seeing the bruises had just stepped up her plan.

My dad had gone for a business meeting out of town for a week, while he was away we packed up our things and left. First going to a motel as we waited for her job transfer to be completed, her boss told us of the house we could rent here. When it was all finalized, we left. The only real thing I left behind was Deke.

Coming back to reality I know the damage that has been done to me is bad, but I am not willing to go to the hospital. I don't want my mom to drag me away from my new life, I don't want her to drag me away from Nate, and especially Marcus.

"Just take me to your place, please," I beg, looking at Nate, he nods.

CHAPTER THIRTY-NINE

Marcus

Pulling in front of Rachel's house, I spot Jackson's car moving up beside mine. Jumping from my Jeep, Rachel rushes inside, Jackson hot on her heels. Taking my time, I exit my Jeep wanting nothing more than to jump back in and return to the diner. But I know what would happen if I did. I'd be outed; Rachel would make mine and Trey's lives a living hell.

Slumping my shoulders, I head them inside, following their voices to the den. Dropping on the couch I say nothing, just stare off into space. Trey's face keeps appearing before me, the tightness in my chest almost choking me.

Pulling out my cell I look at the screen, hoping for something, anything to let me know that he is okay, but it remains blank. Dropping my phone to the couch, I watch as they both laugh, Rachel sitting on Jackson's lap rubbing herself against him.

When my eyes lock with hers, she smiles, a grin that reminds me of the Cheshire Cat. Jackson reaches around her, pawing at her breasts and she lets out these tiny fake moans, urging him on. His hands creep down to her waistband, unbuttoning the fly on her jeans and disappearing inside. I should be disgusted, but instead, I feel defeated.

Tilting her head to the side, Rachel's eyes remain on mine as Jackson does God knows what to her. Her moans grow louder.

"Did he almost tempt you, Marcus? I know I said you told him no and he did that," motioning to my face. The bruises she knows I didn't get from Trey, but has led others to believe I did, "but were you close? Did you wonder what it would feel like for someone to fuck you in the ass?"

Grinding her pussy against Jackson's hand, I can see the fire in her eyes. I refrain from answering, her words not fully registering. Pulling away from Jackson and standing abruptly, Rachel makes her way over to me. Unbuttoning her top as she does, letting it flutter to the floor.

Moving her hands to the waist of her jeans she pushes them to the floor, toeing off her shoes and stepping out of them. Standing before me in just her bra and lacy panties, in the past, it would have left me hard, but now I'm just repulsed.

"If you're wondering what it's like, maybe I'll let you sink that glorious cock of yours into me." Reaching her hand back to Jackson he joins her, his fingers unclasping her bra and letting it fall to the floor before grabbing at her breasts again, tweaking her nipples.

"Maybe as a reward, I'll let you both fuck me at the same time." Rachel pushes her ass back into Jackson and he groans. Like a light bulb going off inside her head, "Jackson, baby, you'd do anything for me right?"

Nodding eagerly Jackson peppers kisses down her neck to her shoulder and I look away. Why is she making me watch this? "Anything for you babe."

"I want you to give Marcus his first time, I want you to fuck him, while he fucks me." Jackson's eyes widen and I look on in abject horror. "We can always use a blindfold. You can imagine it's my ass you're fucking. He wanted Trey to fuck him, so why not you?"

The realization suddenly hits me like a ton of bricks and my jaw drops as I finally listen to her words; Jackson knows more than he's saying. If he knows that Trey isn't the one that hurt me, does he know who actually did? What did Rachel offer him, to get him to do her bidding?

Scrambling off the couch, I charge past them both and straight out of the front door in the direction of my Jeep. Jumping in, I'm tearing out of there before I've even let the door fully close. I know I can't go to Trey's, but I don't have to stay here.

CHAPTER FORTY

Trey

I t takes us a while to get me cleaned up, I keep looking at my cell hoping that Marcus will text or call but I get nothing. Thankfully, Nate's mom isn't home so there's no one to ask any questions. I'm left with a busted lip, two black eyes, and a patchwork of bruises across my chest, sides, and back.

I tell Nate everything that I remember, from going to the diner with Marcus, Rachel appearing, and then heading to the restroom. Before being hit in the back of the head and dragged out to the alley, where Jackson and his friends set themselves on me.

I recall the things they'd said about me, the names, and how it sounded like they thought I was the one who attacked Marcus. Nate hadn't asked about the marks when he'd seen them on Marcus the day before, and I hadn't felt it was my place to tell him.

But now after this, I needed him to know that it wasn't me. Of course, he believed me, telling me he couldn't imagine I'd do anything like that. When I told him it was Marcus' dad

Nate's mouth dropped open, he just couldn't understand it, even though he knew my own story.

After sending a quick text to my mom letting her know I'm okay and that I'm staying at Nate's. I stretch out on the guest bed holding my side. Looking at my cell again I suck in a deep breath, God even breathing hurts. I open a new message to Marcus.

Are you okay? Where are you? Yeah, I might be the one nursing injuries right now, but I'm worried about him. I can't phantom why he just left me there, what happened after I blacked out? I stare at my cell waiting on a response but still nothing.

Fuck it, scrolling through my contacts I find Marcus' number and hit call. My whole body is twitching, I just need him to answer but it just rings and rings before going to voicemail.

"Marcus, where are you? I'm okay but I need you to call me. I need to know you're okay." I sound desperate but I don't care. Placing my phone on my chest, I close my eyes trying to breathe through the pain wracking my body.

When my cell phone rings, I grab at it and see Marcus' name flash up on the screen. I fumble in my urgency to answer.

"Marcus! Where are you?" I pant, the sound of female laughter and a moan on the other end sets me on edge all of a sudden.

"I'm sorry Trey, Marcus can't come to the phone right now." It's Rachel, what the fuck is she doing with his phone? Another moan and panting have my fist curling into the sheets. "You see, he's come to his senses finally."

A sharp intake of breath. "And he'll definitely be cumming in me later. You were just a mistake, a lapse in judgement." I can hear a man grunting in the background. If she has his phone, Marcus must be with her. "Now run along if you know what's good for you." With a quick succession of beeps, she ends the call.

I just stare at the black screen of my phone; it feels like someone has wrapped their fist around my heart and is trying to rip it from my chest. I tighten my grip around my cell, launching it across the room. It hits the wall with a thud before falling to the floor.

How could he do this to me? I thought this was the start of something. But instead, he'd taken his fill of me, and as soon as Rachel came crawling back he slithered straight back into her bed. I just stare at the ceiling,

Nate has told me I couldn't sleep for at least a few more hours, in case of a concussion. But at this very moment, I just want the blackness to take me, I don't even care if I don't come back from it.

CHAPTER FORTY-ONE

Marcus

Waking as the sun rises, I reach for my phone but find it's not there. The previous day comes flooding back to me in a rush. The diner, Trey laid on the floor blood covering his face, and the smug look on Rachel's face. Then back at Rachel's, and her telling Jackson she wanted him to fuck me.

Jackson now knows I like guys, and the very thought of that terrifies me. I don't want others to know, I'm not ready for that. I don't want Trey to get hurt again. I'll have to play into Rachel's little game for now, bide my time, and hope I don't lose Trey in the process.

My head is all over the place, and all I want to do is text Trey and find out if he's okay, but I don't have a clue where my phone is. I remember looking at it the night before at Rachel's but after that, I can't remember what happened to it.

A hammering at the door makes me jump. The door crashes open smacking back against the wall, and Franklin barges inside.

"Rise and shine sunshine! It's another week of hell!" Franklin hollers, his loud voice making my ears ring. "Get your ass in the shower and make sure your cock is shining for the ladies."

I haven't told him much of what has happened since he saw me last on Friday at the movies, only that my dad and I had gotten into another disagreement and I needed somewhere to crash until he calmed down.

Not telling him a single thing about Trey or even my feelings for him; nothing. I can't. If I do, I can't even start to imagine what Rachel would do. So far only her, my family, and her lap dog Jackson know the real truth of what's going on.

"I'm moving, now fuck off!" I smirk at Franklin, and he blows me a kiss, before spinning and walking away down the hall.

Rising from the bed I make my way to the bathroom, throwing myself into the shower before the water has even heated, cleaning myself as quickly as possible. Thank God for my spare clothes at Franklin's, I wore a few of Trey's while his mom washed mine for me, but now I need something different to wear.

With the towel slung around my hips, I make my way into Franklin's bedroom, and straight into the closet. When I exit my eyes fall on the bathroom where Trey and I had shared our first kiss. Pushing the memory away, I quickly walk with the clothes in hand to the guest room and get ready.

Stomping down the stairs, I head straight out the front door to my Jeep where Franklin is already waiting for me. Getting inside we both buckle up before I start the engine and pull out of his drive, my eyes fall on my house as we pull out.

Thoughts of my dad come to mind again, the hatred in his eyes and his threats were terrifying, between him and Rachel, they could both make my life absolute hell.

Franklin for once is quiet the entire way to school, which

is definitely unlike him but I have nothing to say to him right now. If I speak, I won't be able to stop. I'll tell him eventually.

When we pull into the school parking lot, Rachel is waiting for me. Jackson is stood to her side, much closer than he needs to be, but neither of them seems to care. I get out of the Jeep, keeping my eyes down, and grab my backpack.

Making my way over to them I stop and look at her, I wish looks could kill. If they could, right now Rachel would be dead.

"Oh, don't look so angry Marcus, we're both getting what we want. I get you, and you get to keep your secrets." Walking closer to her, she runs her hand up my chest. "I have something for you," reaching into her bag she pulls out my cell phone, and hands it to me.

Snatching it from her I check my calls and texts, but there's nothing there. The last text is the one I sent to Nate asking him to find Trey. I was hoping maybe there would be something to confirm Trey is okay, but there's nothing.

"Now we better get inside, remember to make it look good Marcus. Your secrets depend on it, and I guess, so does Trey's safety." Taking my hand in hers, she leads me toward the school, a thousand thoughts are running through my head.

I don't know if I can do this, keep up this sick game, and give Rachel all the control. Everything in me is telling me to shrug her off and walk away. To just deal with the consequences as they come. Maybe I can stand up for Trey, protect him. We could protect each other.

But I push those thoughts away, if playing Rachel's game is what will protect him right now, then that's what I'm going to have to do. Even if it chips away at little pieces of my heart every day. I'll do it for him.

CHAPTER FORTY-TWO

Trey

I tell Nate about the phone call last night, as he drives me to my house to pick up my backpack and change my clothes. Even he is shocked at how quickly Marcus had gone back to that crazy bitch. He keeps looking into Marcus' apology, telling me there has to be more to it.

My mom's still in bed when we arrive so I sneak inside, tip-toeing to my room to change out of my filthy clothes and swiping my bag from the hallway before hobbling back out to Nate's car.

Arriving at school, Nate kills the engine and I just sit in there taking calming breaths. Everything still hurts but I popped a couple of Tylenol before breakfast, and I'm hoping they kick in soon.

"Are you sure you're ready to do this? I can drive you back to mine, get my mom to cover for you."

Ignoring Nate, I push myself out of the car and grab my bag from the foot well. Holding my head high, I don't even wait for Nate. I might look like shit, but I'm not going to let Marcus take anything else from me. He's already taken my heart, so at this point what else is there to take?

When I walk through the double doors all the conversations seem to stop. Students who I've never even spoken to before, and those I have, just stare at me. Then the whispering starts, more insults because of my sexuality and the state of my face are hissed at me, but I ignore them all as I make my way to my locker.

"Did you hear what happened between him and Marcus?" A voice not that far from me sounds and it makes me cringe.

"Rachel said he tried to force himself on Marcus, cornered him or something." Another voice chimes.

"Yeah, but Jackson found out and they all taught him a lesson. Even Marcus got a few kicks in." Says another.

"Serves him right, we don't need his kind round here trying to steal our guys!" Laughter follows them, as they make their way down the hall.

What the actual fuck is going on? What exactly have Rachel and Marcus been telling people, if he wanted me to leave him alone, why didn't he just tell me? It would have hurt, but I would have walked away. Or at least I'd have tried to.

My chest tightens, and I can feel myself getting dizzy. A hand on my shoulder has me almost jumping out of my skin, I turn and see Nate standing behind me.

"Trey, you need to breathe. If you don't, you're going to pass out." Moving to the side of me he blocks some of the stares I can feel piercing into me.

"I'm fine Nate!" I snarl, slamming my locker closed. By the sounds of it, Marcus has moved on, Rachel may be the one who said I forced myself on him, but now he's found the perfect way out of it. It sounds like he may have even gotten a few kicks in himself just to cover his own back.

Turning, I storm away heading for class, as I near I spot some of the jocks and cheerleaders leaning against their own lockers. In the middle of the group stands Marcus and

Rachel. He has his arm slung around her shoulder as she kisses his cheek.

When she spots me, she licks her lips and blows me a kiss. The group bursts out laughing. Marcus doesn't even look at me, keeping his gaze on Rachel as she whispers into his ear. I think he looks up at the last second, but I just keep walking.

"Homo!"

"Gay boy!"

"Faggot!" The calls follow me down the hall. A teacher stepping out of a classroom has them soon quietening down.

"We do not accept that sort of language in this school. Now get to class before I give you all detention!" Looking at the teacher as I stride past, he throws me a weak smile but all I can do is scowl.

Walking into class, I ignore the stares and comments and grab an empty table in the back corner of the classroom, as far away from the other students as I can. I'll just keep my head down, I'll get through the day. I'm not sure exactly what's going to happen after that.

At some point, I'm going to have to go home, but for now, I can tell my mom Nate and I need to work on our project for a few days until some of the swelling has gone down. Hell, I'll stick ice on my face every day if that helps.

I know deep down I can't let her see me like this, not again. But with her shifts at work, I should be able to mostly avoid her. If she asks about Marcus, I'll just tell her he went back home. I couldn't care less where he's staying at this point. Marcus Brady is not my problem anymore.

CHAPTER FORTY-THREE

Marcus

It's nearly two weeks after what happened and my heart breaks every time a name is thrown at Trey across the halls of the school, but I feel utterly powerless to do anything about it. The hurt is written all over his face, but he tries to school his expression before anyone sees it, but I always catch it.

My parents are beyond ecstatic that Rachel and I are *back together,* and my dad even said I could come home as long as I don't disgrace him again. I went back once while they weren't home to grab some more clothes, before setting up camp at Franklin's.

I'm eighteen now, so there isn't much my parents can say or do about my new living circumstances, and even if they cut me off, I still have money in savings as well as some inheritance from my grandparents. I am even looking around town for jobs after school.

Rachel is getting worse. Every time she wants something, her threats of outing me and my fear of Trey getting hurt again come to light. She constantly reminds me of those threats again when she catches me looking Trey's way.

She's made me give her oral, and finger fuck her till she cums. Even used the threats if I didn't let her give me a blow job. I just close my eyes through the entire experience pretending instead it is someone else's mouth around my dick.

When I cum, she thinks it is for her, but it isn't. I fuck her mouth until I cum, letting her choke on my dick as rope after rope of my release shoots down her throat. Imagining Trey has his lips around me, even if the feel of it is missing a lip ring.

It took her less than a week before she demanded I fuck her, telling me if I don't she will tell my dad more about Trey, where he lives, and that the only reason we are back together is so I can hide the fact I'm actually gay. The look I get when I tell her I think I'm actually bisexual makes it so much worse.

So here I am with my dick buried in her pussy as she rides me. I can't help the moans that slip from my mouth, but I close my eyes tight trying to imagine that it is anyone but her I'm with. Rachel grabs onto my nipples and twists them, the pain jolting through my system. The complete opposite of when Trey sucked on them.

Fisting my hair in her hand she tries to drag my lips to hers but at the last second, I manage to turn my head and kiss down her neck sucking on the skin there. I know I'll leave a bruise but I don't care. Scrapping my teeth over her pulse she thrashes about in my lap. Twisting and turning on my dick.

Reaching between us I push my thumb over her clit, I want her to finish, I need her to finish. Then at least she will leave, she'll have had her way with me, and probably go back to fucking Jackson. I know she's still screwing around with him, but it doesn't bother me anymore. I wish she'd just take him completely and leave me the hell alone.

Flicking at her clit, her pussy tightens around me. Throwing back her head, Rachel cries out, her pussy tightening even further but I don't cum. Pushing her from me, I stand abruptly and walk into the bathroom to dispose of the condom before she realizes.

When I reach the bathroom door she's already tugging her clothing back on, she looks at my still hard cock and saunters toward me.

"Are you ready for round two already? I can always tell Jackson I'm running a little late." The smirk on her face makes me scowl.

"I'm good, you can show yourself out." Slamming the door in her face I lock it and turn, leaning back on it, expelling all the air from my lungs. I rest my head back against it, looking at the ceiling, and sigh.

I don't know how much longer I can do this, she's using me for her own reasons. She's obsessed with me. When will this ever end? I don't know how much more my heart can take. My dreams are plagued every night by Trey, of all our encounters.

From the pool party, to turning up at his place after the fight with my dad, to seeing him lying on the floor covered in blood. Clenching my fists tight, my short nails dig into the palms of my hands. At some point, enough is going to have to be enough.

I can't continue letting Rachel dictate what I do and using her threats to make sure she gets my compliance as she uses and abuses my body for her own pleasure. Trying to clear my mind, I move to the shower and turn on the water.

Stepping under the cold spray before it's even heated, I start to scrub my body in an attempt to get every trace of Rachel off my skin, leaving it bright red. When I'm happy with my progress, I lean back on the shower wall and sink to the floor, resting my head against the cold tiles.

Closing my eyes, my mind drifts again to Trey. All the kisses, smiles, and experiences he gave me, even in the short time we spent together. I'd do anything to be near him again, to touch him. When the water once again goes cold, I stand, struggling to move my now stiff limbs.

Pulling a towel down from the rack I dry my body, leaving my hair dripping. Staggering back into the bedroom, I find the room empty of Rachel. Thankfully she listened to my words and left. Shutting the bedroom door, I close and lock it, I'm not taking any risks.

Moving to the bed I don't even bother to put boxers on before I lie down, pulling the sheet over me and closing my eyes.

My dream is different this time. I see Trey in an empty room dressed in a suit, walking toward him cautiously hoping that he won't just disappear. When I reach him, he turns and smiles. Wrapping his arms around me he pulls me against his body and sways to music only he seems to hear. He moves his lips to mine but before they can touch, I jolt awake.

Morning has come far too quickly and I just want to close my eyes and go back to my dream of Trey. Only I want it to be real. Like a light bulb going off in my mind, I sit bolt upright. A plan is forming in my mind, but I might need a little help.

Grabbing my phone from the drawers, I shoot off a quick text to the one person I'm going to need to accomplish my plan.

CHAPTER FORTY-FOUR

Trey

I want to be anywhere but here, but after Nate incessantly bugged me about it, I ultimately caved. I don't even know why he was so insistent that I came here tonight. Looking around the gym, which now looks like a snow-covered forest, I sip my punch. My gaze falls on Franklin, he's sitting at a table, his arm slung around Jessica's shoulders as she giggles at something he has said.

Chelsey and Jackson are on the dance floor, grinding together like they are having sex right there. Nate is by the punch bowl grabbing another drink, I'm not surprised with the amount of dancing he's been doing.

Keeping to the shadows, I continue to people watch. The bruises from the beating are mostly gone now, but I still don't want to be seen. Continuing to let my gaze roam the crowd, I notice the lack of Marcus and Rachel and wonder where they've gotten to. No doubt she's dragged him off somewhere to give him a blow job. The sting in my chest leaves me gasping.

I'm still not over him, I don't think I ever will be. But I'm also not sure I can ever forgive him for what happened. He just left me, and went running back to Rachel. I thought we had something going on between us. I've never felt so connected to someone before. For two days, he was totally mine.

But he left me, the darkness has gripped around my heart leaving me empty inside. Seeing them in school, Rachel is always all over him, and Marcus acting like I didn't even exist anymore, has broken me. Heat suddenly covers my back, his scent filling my nostrils.

"Dance with me..." Marcus' lips whisper over the skin on my neck sending shivers down my spine, his fingers lacing with my own. Ripping myself away, I turn and face him. My eyes settle on his blue ones.

"What do you want, Marcus?" My words are harsh, "Are you here to torment me some more?" Stepping closer to me, his hand reaches toward my cheek. When I feel the heat, I pull away again.

"I'm not here for that Trey, I can't do this anymore." I can see the upset in his eyes, but what does he have to be upset about? It's my heart he ripped out.

"Just leave me alone Marcus, haven't you done enough already?" I stalk away, leaving my glass on a table as I pass. I spot Franklin watching me, his eyes shifting behind me.

As I storm out of the double doors and out of the gym, I've made my decision, I'm getting the hell out of here. I feel bad for leaving Nate, but I can't stay here, I'll text him on the way home.

"Trey, please wait." Marcus' voice calls behind me, but I keep going. A hand on my shoulder stops me in my tracks and I spin, my fists raised. "Please...I'm sorry." Marcus holds his hands in front of him in a peaceful gesture, but I'm still on guard.

"What are you sorry for Marcus? For leading me on? For

making me think you cared? For helping your friends kick the crap out of me?" My voice raises with each question.

"I didn't...I never..." Marcus' voice cracks as he speaks. "I never touched you, Trey. Rachel told me if I didn't walk away, she'd tell everyone about me, about us. She'd let Jackson carry on. They would have killed you!"

Laughter barks out of me, "So instead you ripped out my heart, left me there, and went straight back to her without a word. It certainly sounded like you'd forgotten me when Rachel called me on your phone." Marcus' face drops, his eyes widening.

"My phone... What did she say, Trey?" he steps closer to me but I back away.

"That you'd come to your senses, and you'd be filling her with your cum later. I could hear you in the background, and her moans were definitely real." I remember her words and it tears at my heart all over again.

"That wasn't me Trey. I took her home that night, Jackson followed. When we went inside, she was all over him, she stripped, told Jackson to fuck me while I fucked her. I left." I blink at him; his words sound so unbelievable. If it's true, then Rachel really does have no boundaries.

I side-step, leaning on the lockers lining the hallway, my brain is reeling from the new information. Rolling slightly so my back is against the lockers, I lean back letting my head drop back onto them, and close my eyes.

She ruined everything, I'm angry at her, I'm angry at Marcus, I'm hurt, I'm sad. Nate had said there had to be more to it than I thought, but I couldn't see it. I listened to the rumors, letting them fill in the blanks from that night along with the phone call.

Marcus steps closer to me again, I can feel the heat of his body close but not quite touching. When I open my eyes, I can see the sadness in his, mirroring my own.

"Please Trey, I'm so sorry." Lifting his hand, he runs his fingers up my cheek whispering over the lingering bruise just under my eye. This time I can't resist and my head tilts, pushing against his hand. His eyes flicker to my mouth before moving back to my eyes. "I need you, Trey. I'll always need you."

Pushing his body against mine, our lips connect, and I can't help the small moan that escapes me. I've missed his heat, the softness of his lips against my own, the way he holds me. Wrapping my arms around his waist, I pull his body flush with mine.

Our tongues tangle and his hand disappears into my hair, keeping my lips tight against his. We swallow each other's moans, our bodies rubbing together. Marcus breaks the kiss, our eyes opening and locking together. Both our chests are heaving.

Running his hand down my arm he interlocks our fingers pulling me away from the lockers. Thinking we will leave, I'm shocked when he instead starts pulling me back to the gym.

"Marcus, where are we going?" I stumble trying to bring him to a stop, but he carries on.

"Trust me," pushing through the double doors he drags me inside.

CHAPTER FORTY-FIVE

Marcus

With his hand firmly encased in mine, I walk into the dance with my head held up high. A few people look up at us as we pass, their eyes lingering on us. Their voices whispered. As we approach the dance floor, I spot Rachel dirty dancing with Jackson. Chelsey stands at the edge throwing daggers at them both.

When Rachel spots us, I can see the emotions that pass across her face as she takes in our joined hands. First, the look of shock, which slowly turns to anger. Pushing Jackson from her, she stomps over and stops in front of us, blocking the way to the dance floor.

"What the fuck is this Marcus? Are you drunk? Is that why you're letting him," her eyes hone in on Trey, "touch you?" Folding her arms across her chest, Jackson stalks up behind her.

"Need me to teach him another lesson baby?" Jackson narrows his eyes on Trey, eager to do her bidding.

"What I need is for you to both get the fuck out of my way!" My voice is stern.

"It doesn't matter Marcus, let's just go." Trey tugs on my

hand, wanting to pull me away but I stand my ground. The couples on the dance floor have stopped dancing, we have garnered everyone's attention at this point.

"Actually, it does matter. Move Rachel, I want to dance with my boyfriend." A few gasps sound around me, including Trey's. When I look over my shoulder at him, he's just staring at me, his mouth open.

Shoving past Rachel and Jackson, I pull Trey onto the dance floor and pull him against me. Every set of eyes is on us, but I'm past caring. These last few weeks have been the worst of my life, and I refuse to let the fear of being outed trap me any longer.

A screech that could rival that of a banshee sounds from over my shoulder and I glance to the side as Rachel storms off the dance floor, Jackson is close on her heels. My gaze falls on Franklin and he just grins, giving me a thumbs up. His reaction throws me, but I'll ask him about that later.

Looping my hands around Trey's neck, his hands rest on my waist. We're standing close, but it's not enough for me and I pull him closer, swaying to the music. Everything around us disappears and it leaves only Trey and me.

With his body this close to me, I, at long last, feel like I'm home. Like I'm where I'm meant to be. A part of me has been missing for so long, and I realize now that part was Trey. He completes me.

Ignoring the gazes burning into me, I pull Trey's lips toward me. When they connect, I can't stifle the moan that escapes me. I run my tongue over the ring in Trey's lip and he opens up for me. Pushing my tongue inside his mouth, I rub it along his.

Hands on my shoulders rip me away from Trey, and Jackson stands between us his fists raised. I can feel the anger radiating from him. I'm not even sure why, what has my sexuality got to do with him. Looking into his eyes, they narrow.

As if in slow motion his fist starts to swing in my direction, I know I won't have time to move but I just stand my ground. Before his fist can connect, he suddenly disappears from in front of me. Another body colliding with him.

Time speeds up again as Franklin tackles Jackson and shoves him back. Jackson stumbles, falling into Rachel. His weight takes her back, straight into the table with the punch on it. As they fall, the table crashes down to the ground with them. The entire bowl of punch pouring over them both.

Rachel looks like something out of Carrie, her white dress stained with red liquid. There's utter silence around us, the music has cut off. Sitting in the puddle of liquid, Rachel flails trying to get purchase on the floor to stand, but she keeps slipping. Jackson isn't faring much better.

A bark of laughter sounds behind me, then another, then a whole chorus of people are laughing all around me. They point and laugh, as they watch Rachel finally taken down a step or two. Franklin approaches me and rests his hand on my shoulder.

"Thanks." What else can I say to him? He stopped Jackson so spectacularly and took both him and Rachel out in the process.

"What are friends for? Now you two," his eyes shift to Trey, "better get out of here before the teachers descend. Go enjoy yourselves. This dance is a drag anyway." Franklin walks away leaving me stunned once more. The teachers chaperoning the dance, who seemed to be missing when Jackson took a swing, finally rush over to help him and Rachel up off the floor.

Trey slips his hand into mine and we turn, slipping through the gathered crowd and walk out of the dance. Nate stands off to the side and he's beaming, he nods at us as we pass. When we get out of the doors, Trey's grip on my hand tightens as he drags me to the exit.

Walking out to the car park, I pull in the direction of my Jeep, I don't want to let go of Trey. Not now that I have him again. But our hands move apart as we both climb into my Jeep. Starting the engine, I look over at Trey and we both burst out laughing.

It's been a strange night for sure, I didn't plan on it going quite this way. I'd gone to the dance with Rachel, planning to let her think I was playing my part. Though secretly I'd made arrangements with Nate for him to get Trey there. I wanted to end it with Rachel once and for all in front of witnesses, to tell them what she'd done. But seeing Trey in the shadows, I couldn't deny the pull between us and I acted sooner.

We eventually manage to calm ourselves and I pull out of the car park, I reach to Trey as I drive and his fingers lock with mine. Looking at him out of the corner of my eye, I see the smile I've missed so much pulling up his lips.

CHAPTER FORTY-SIX

Trey

Reaching across the console I take his hand in mine, our fingers lock together. Bringing his hand to my mouth, I run my lips across his knuckles before leaving a kiss there. The drive is silent after our laughing fit, but we keep looking at each other. The smile on his face is perfect.

"Marcus...I..." I whisper. Marcus pulls up outside my house and we just sit there, our fingers still entwined.

"Shhh Trey, I want this. I'm glad they all know, no more hiding." Using my hand to pull me across to him, his lips leave the softest kiss on mine, before he pulls back. We both get out of his Jeep and head to the front door, hand in hand. Opening the door, we walk inside.

Mom isn't home again, she's having a girl's night with Sharon, expecting I'd be gone most of the night. When the door is closed, I push Marcus back against it. My hands tangle in his hair, and I guide his lips to mine. Our kisses are heated, and I'm so hard, my cock is straining against the fabric of my slacks.

Pushing a leg between Marcus' I rub my thigh against his hardening length, and he moans, my own cock pushing against his thigh. Without parting our lips, I pull him back away from the door and back up to the stairs.

Turning I walk up them, kicking my shoes off as I go, Marcus is directly behind me. His hand squeezes my ass as I climb the stairs, when we reach the top, I lead him to my room. Entering I shrug out of my suit jacket and throw it over the back of the chair.

Pulling Marcus to me using the lapels of his jacket, I kiss him again, and push the jacket from his shoulders. Keeping our lips connected, we start to unbutton each other's shirts. Fumbling slightly as our hands get in each other's way.

Laughing we eventually manage it. Pulling apart we just stare at each other, drinking in every detail of each other. We've seen each other in various states of undress before, but this time it feels different. Shrugging out of our shirts we discard them on the floor.

My fingers trace up Marcus' abdominal muscles, skimming over his flesh, making him tremble as goosebumps erupt over his skin, showing just how sensitive he is to my touch. Dropping to my knees before him, I revel in the way his blue eyes follow me down, I unbuckle his belt and deftly undo the button and zipper. As it pulls over his hard cock, he lets out a groan.

Gripping the waistband of his boxers and slacks, I pull them down his legs, Marcus' cock springs up bobbing up and down in front of my face and I lick my lips. Wrapping his hard length with my hand, I stroke him a few times before running my tongue over the swollen head.

His cock jumps as I wrap my mouth around him drawing him deep. Bobbing up and down on his steely length, Marcus seizes my hair guiding himself deeper between my lips. I flatten my tongue. The head of his cock pushes on the back of my throat and I swallow him down.

His fingers tighten in my hair. I push and push, wanting to

drive him to the edge of insanity. My hands grab onto his ass cheeks and I squeeze, digging my fingers into his flesh. Pulling back from his cock, I let him drop from my mouth.

I make the journey slowly back up his body kissing and nipping every inch of him I can lay my mouth on, his moans and groans urging me on. Licking around his nipple I run my teeth over the stiff peak, his moans are music to my ears. I want him so bad, every one of my nerve endings is tingling.

Undoing my slacks, I push them and my boxers down my legs and step out of them. We stand before each other, our eyes roving over each other's naked bodies. My cock twitches and I wrap my hand around it. Pumping it a few times.

Laying my hands on Marcus' shoulders, I push him back slowly until the back of his knees hit the edge of my bed. Wrapping my hand around the back of his neck, I pull his mouth to mine. Running my tongue along the seam of his lips, he opens for me.

Our tongues battle together, and my hands move to his sides, tracing across his skin. Marcus grabs my ass and pulls our bodies together, our cocks touching and rubbing against each other. His mouth breaks away from mine and he trails his lips down my skin, over my sensitive flesh.

Licking down the tattoo on my chest, Marcus takes my pierced nipple into his mouth, grasping the pieced tip between his teeth. I tangle my fingers into his hair, holding his mouth to me as his tongue flicks over my nipple.

Moans escape from between my parted lips. Moving to my other nipple, Marcus gives it the same treatment that he gave the other. Fisting my cock, he runs his hand up and down my hard length, moving over the top of my pierced head. I gasp.

Moving down my body Marcus sits, his face is now in line with my cock. Leaning forward he runs his tongue over my sensitive head, and I shiver. Sucking me into his mouth he goes to town, his tongue swirling around me, his hand squeezing my balls.

Removing his mouth from me, he takes my cock in his hand lifting it so he can suck my balls. Licking me from base to tip, he encases me once more in his mouth. My gasps and moans, and the sound of his wet mouth sucking on me, are the only noises in the silent house.

With my fingers running through his hair, my hips buck, thrusting my cock into Marcus' mouth and brushing up against the back of his throat. Relaxing around my shaft, he takes me all the way in, deep throating me before pulling back again.

His hands move to my ass, he squeezes my cheeks, and I continue to thrust in and out of his mouth. As my cock moves out of his mouth, he swirls his tongue around the head before taking me in deep again. If I carry on like this, chances are I'm going to cum.

My cock pulls out of Marcus' mouth with a pop and he looks up at me licking over his lips. His pupils are blown, and he's panting. His cock is bobbing against his abs. Resting my hands on his shoulders, I push him back on the bed so he's laid down.

Walking to the drawers beside my bed I open it, pulling out a bottle of lube and a box of condoms. Marcus' eyes track my every move and when he sees what I've grabbed, he draws in a deep breath. Moving back to Marcus I deposit the items on the bed and take up his knees pulling his ass to the end of the bed, leaving his knees bent up.

Picking up the lube I squeeze some out onto his puckered hole and drop the bottle back down. He seemed to enjoy it last time I'd fingered him, but this time, I need to prepare him for taking my cock. Running my fingers through the lube, I rub it around his anus.

Slowly I push one finger inside, reaching the first knuckle.

Marcus bucks against the intrusion, his head moving from side to side. When he stops moving, I push in even further until my whole finger is inside him. Taking my time I work my finger in and out of him, before adding another.

Scissoring my fingers with the aim to widen him. Taking his cock in my other hand I work it and my fingers in tandem. The groans coming from Marcus' lips turn me on even further, my own cock twitching with each sound.

CHAPTER FORTY-SEVEN

Marcus

With his fingers inside me and his hand wrapped around my dick, Trey is pushing me higher and higher. The pleasure ripples through my body, my breathing is harsh. I'm almost gasping as I try and drag oxygen into my lungs.

Trey's fingers pull out of my anus abruptly, and I whine at the sudden feeling of emptiness. He reaches for a condom out of the box. Sitting up I grab it from him, and I smile. Ripping it open using my teeth, I take his dick in my hand and sheath him in the latex. Taking up the lube bottle, I squirt it onto my palm, and wrap my fingers around his cock.

Working the lubricant up and down his shaft, I make sure every inch of him is covered. Laying back on the bed, I open my legs for him, and Trey steps between them. He squirts more lube around my tight hole and rubs the head of his dick through it.

Holding my breath, Trey's dick pushes past the tight ring of muscle aided by the lube coating us both, my fists grasp onto his sheets at the sharp sting. He's taking it slow, making sure he doesn't hurt me. Inch by inch he sinks in, his piercing rubbing against me in the most delicious way. My mouth falls open and I squeeze my eyes shut.

When he's halfway inside me he stops, his breathing is heavy. Moving fully over me, his arms on either side of my head holding him above me. He leans down between my open legs and kisses me, pushing his dick a little further into me, and we swallow each other's gasps.

My dick bounces against his abs. I need him to move. Using my feet, I wrap them behind his ass and drag him toward me until he's fully seated inside. I feel so full and it's glorious, my ass relaxes around his width and any pain I initially felt disappears and turns to pleasure.

"I need you to move Trey." I drag out between pants.

Slowly Trey pulls his dick out so only the head remains, before thrusting back in with a grunt. His movements are slow and steady as he thrusts in and out of me. His piercing constantly rubs all the right places.

"More..." I moan out biting on my lower lip. Trey's eyes lock on mine.

The moans escaping my mouth must urge Trey on because he starts to pick up the speed of his thrusts. Covering my own dick with my fist, I squeeze and pump it up and down, the levels of pleasure I'm feeling, are coursing through my body, all the way to my toes.

Pulling my leg up to his shoulder changes the entire angle and I groan. Trey's pace quickens further and so does my hand working up and down my dick. I'm so close now and can only hope that Trey is too. His thrusts begin to falter, and I can feel my balls tightening.

We both roar our releases. My hot cum splatters all over my stomach. Trey thrusts a few more times inside my ass, riding out the last of his orgasm before stilling. With his dick still inside me, Trey leans down and captures my lips, thrusting his tongue inside my mouth.

My heart is racing as we trade kisses. When he pulls back from me, Trey looks into my eyes.

"I love you," he whispers.

"I love you too." And I mean every word, I've never once told a partner I've loved them before. Yes, I've cared about them, but most of the time we just fucked, we never made love like Trey and I just did.

As his dick softens, he pulls out of me and I feel empty again. Disappearing into the bathroom, he returns without the condom and a cloth in his hand. Trey wipes away my cum from my stomach, before wiping the lube from around my ass.

Throwing the cloth into the hamper, he takes my hand in his and pulls me up from the bed. My legs still feel a little like jello but I manage to hold my own weight. Before he can tug me to the bathroom, I grab the bottle of lube and a few more condoms. Trey looks at me with a raised eyebrow when he sees what's in my hand.

"Just in case." Trey lets out a soft laugh at my comment before pulling me into the bathroom.

Memories of the night I turned up on his doorstep flash in my mind. Remembering how Trey had taken care of me in my time of need.

When we get inside, he releases my hand and turns on the shower, before stepping under the spray. Roving my eyes over his back and his ass have my dick twitching again. Placing the items on the shelf just inside, I step up behind him.

Running my lips down the side of his neck I nip at his skin, tasting the sweat that still lingers on his flesh. Grabbing the soap, I move it up and down his back lathering him up. Stepping closer, I reach around the front of him, my hardening dick rubbing between his ass cheeks, and he pushes back into me.

Taking hold of the back of my hair, Trey turns his head

and kisses me, nipping at my lip and making me moan as my dick pushes against his ass. Stepping back, I drop the soap, grab a condom and sheath my steel length inside it. Grabbing the lube, I run my hands up and down my length.

I've never been so quick to recover from an orgasm before, but now that I've felt Trey inside me. I want nothing more than to feel his ass squeezing around my dick. The thought of it makes me harder, if that's even possible. Placing a hand on the center of Trey's back, I push him forward until he rests his hands on the tiled wall in front of him, his ass pushed back.

Grabbing the lube, I run my hands up and down my length. With the lube still coating my fingers, I push one inside Trey and he moans. Thrusting my finger in and out of him before I push another in. His hips push back into my hand. Grasping on to his ass with my other hand I squeeze and slap his cheek.

When I think he's ready, I pull my fingers from him, and run my dick up and down his crack, while squeezing his cheek still with my other hand. Lining my dick up with his hole, I push inside. Trey's hips rock back taking me in further.

With my dick fully seated inside him, I take a few deep breaths, adjusting to the feel of him around my hard length. When I think we're both comfortable, I withdraw before pushing back in with short, shallow thrusts.

"Harder Marcus." Trey rushes out between moans.

Taking his hips in my hands I slam into him, thrusting in and out with wild abandon. Pulling his hips back to meet me, our moans echo around the bathroom. Trey's fingers curl against the shower wall as my thrusts push him closer to it.

"Fuck yes!" Trey hollers, I can feel myself getting close, so I slow down my movements again. I want to last as long as I can, but Trey doesn't let me slow down for long.

Ramming his hips back to meet mine, he takes matters into his own hands and I can't deny him any longer. Withdrawing almost entirely from his hole I slam back home, my hips crashing into him. I can feel my balls tightening and my dick swelling.

One final thrust is all it takes before I'm coming, emptying my load into the condom. I almost collapse on Trey's back, but he holds my weight up as he straightens. Slipping my arms around him, I hold him against me. His back to my front.

Twisting in my arms my dick slips from his ass, still pulsing from my release. Trey removes the condom and throws it in the trash. Picking up the soap we clean each other, trading soft kisses. When we're both clean, we wrap towels around our hips and help each other dry off.

Leading me back into the bedroom I walk to the other side of the bed, dropping the towel from my hips I crawl under the sheets, as Trey gets in beside me. I'm not sure how I had expected tonight to go but I'm not entirely sure it was like this. I planned to dance with Trey, to beg for his forgiveness.

Not only has he forgiven me, but he has welcomed me back into his life. I don't know what the future has in store for us, but I won't lie or hide who I am anymore. I love Trey, and if I have to, I'll shout it from the rooftops. If people hate me for it then I'll remove them from my life.

Tugging on Trey I pull his back to my chest and wrap my arms around him, his fingers lock with mine, holding my arms tightly around him. Everyone I need in my life is right here in this room, and I don't plan on letting him go any time soon.

EPILOGUE

Marcus

The week after the Winter Formal had been pretty daunting. Trey and I had gotten a few stares when we'd entered school hand in hand on Monday morning but on the whole, people had been pretty accepting. Turns out I didn't need to worry about what Franklin had thought, he already knew. I hadn't even wanted to work out how that had happened, but he was happy for us.

My parents had both disowned me and kicked me out, throwing all my possessions on the front lawn. But with the help of Trey, his mom, Franklin, and Nate, we'd managed to gather everything up and I'd moved in with Trey and his mom.

Turns out she was super cool with us being together and had no issues with us sleeping in the same bed. I'd gotten a job at the diner, thanks to Betsy and Ted, and worked weekends and sometimes after school with the aim to help toward bills. Trey's mom was having none of it though and told me to keep it.

Instead, I dragged Trey to the store with me each week, much to his displeasure to buy groceries. Even though she wouldn't take my money, she couldn't stop me from doing this one little thing in return for her kindness.

Rachel and Jackson had both been suspended from school along with two of the other guys from the football team, none of them completing the school year. According to whispers around school, she'd gotten Jackson to record them beating Trey. Nate had hacked her cloud account and emailed the video to the principal.

With the missing members now on the football team, Trey had informed me about the fact he had played at his old school. I'd marched him straight up to the coach and got him to try out. He'd made it onto the team, and he was actually pretty good.

We won every game till the end of the year. And Trey and I certainly enjoyed cleaning up after the games, we always ended up late to Franklin's parties but when we arrived Franklin always threw us a wink and thumbs up which left Trey and me laughing.

Nate started joining us at the parties too, he'd made a ton of friends but never let anyone steal the spot of his best friend, Trey. At this point, I've seen more of Nate than I ever want to see having walked in on him with one of the cheerleaders. Let's just say he lost something that night.

Even with the crazy final year of high school, Trey and I had both graduated and been accepted to the same college. With money from my inheritance, I'd rented us our own apartment just off the campus and that pretty much brought us up to now.

Unpacking the boxes from the back of my Jeep I lock it and carry them up the stairs. When I get inside, Trey is already starting to empty the ones we've already unloaded in the kitchen. Bent over, reaching into one of the cupboards and humming to himself, my eyes track up his legs to his ass.

Putting the boxes down quietly, I move silently behind

him. Resting my hands on his ass, I squeeze. Jumping Trey shoots up, smacking his head on the inside of the cupboard on the way up. Rubbing the back of his head, he turns on me. Looking less than impressed with me.

"Can't we at least settle in before you try and have your wicked way with me?" he cocks an eyebrow at me as I step toward him pushing him back against the cupboard. He pulls his lip ring between his teeth and my dick pulses.

"Why wait that long? If we want to christen every room, we need to get started." I whisper in his ear, nipping on it. Trey groans.

Rubbing my hardening dick against him, I can feel his straining against the front of his jeans. Trey's hands curl around my hips before he pushes them up under my t-shirt and lifts it over my head. His eyes widen like it's the very first time he's seen me.

Unzipping his jeans, I reach inside, he's going commando again. My hand wraps around his steely length and he jerks in my palm. Trey grips onto the edge of the counter behind him and he closes his eyes. Moving my hand up and down, I use his pre-cum to slicken my movements up and down.

Nipping up his neck, I move up to his mouth and our lips collide, forcing my tongue inside they tangle together, lighting up every single cell in my body. His hips move back and forth, thrusting his dick within the confines of my hand. Trey is panting now, and I tighten my grip on him.

Trey rips his mouth from mine, his eyes are almost black, and it turns me on even more. My dick is so hard now as it pushes against the front of my shorts. Trey removes my hand from his length and laces his fingers with mine dragging me to the couch.

Pushing my shorts and boxers down my hips he lets them drop to the floor before turning me and shoving me down on the couch. He drops to his knees in front of me. Taking my dick in his hand, he gives it a couple of tugs before his mouth wraps around me and I shiver.

I thrust up into his mouth as he bottoms out, my balls smacking on his chin, and my hands gripping his hair. His moans causing vibrations to travel through my entire length. When my dick is covered in his saliva, he removes me from his mouth.

Grabbing the lube from the side table, I run the gel up and down my length before throwing the bottle on the couch.

Kicking his sneakers off, Trey completely removes his jeans and crawls into my lap, our lengths brushing together making us both moan. With his thighs on either side of me, he lifts up grabbing my dick in his hand again. The head nudges against his hole and he sinks down inch by inch.

My balls are already tightening as my dick stretches him, grasping onto me harder than his hand ever could. His fingers sink into the flesh on my shoulders, his whole body is shivering. We work together, I thrust up and he sinks down onto me.

Grabbing his dick, I start to work his length up and down, I want us to cum at the same time and I know I'm already close. Our bodies are both now covered in a fine layer of sweat as we come closer to completion.

With a roar and one final thrust, I'm emptying my hot load inside his ass as his own dick erupts his release across my stomach. Panting, he collapses on top of me and I wrap my arms around him. With our dicks still twitching, mine still inside him. My cum leaking from inside down my thighs.

"Well, that's one room christened." I laugh and Trey joins in. "But we really should clean up. We're meant to be going on a date tonight."

"I know, I know but after hot shower sex, that'll be two rooms, at least." Trey jumps off my lap and heads for the bathroom and I just sit there staring after his sexy ass.

One thing I know is I'll always love Trey Banks, and I'm happy we had that first kiss in Franklin's bathroom. It changed both of our lives forever, for the better. Standing I head for the bedroom, I can hear the shower already running in the bathroom.

Reaching the drawers beside the bed, I open the top drawer moving the socks aside until I find what I'm looking for. Pulling out the box I open it and look at the ring inside. I plan on spending the rest of my life with Trey, if he'll have me.

"Marcus get your ass in here!" Trey hollers from the bathroom.

Shoving the box back in the drawer, I close it and head for the shower and the man I love.

The End

AFTERWORD

This book was a happy accident. A challenge really from an author. I mentioned I used to write fanfiction way back when. They asked if I ever considered publishing, which of course I hadn't. It was never a thought that had crossed my mind because most of my fan-fics were using other people's characters.

I took a look back at some of those old fics and thought maybe, just maybe I could use some of the stuff from those as a starting point for this story. Turns out I didn't need my old stories and what I ended up with was entirely new.

Against the Odds came to life just before NaNoWriMo, but I used the month of November to challenge myself to finish it and I'm glad I did. I hope that anyone who reads this book has enjoyed the characters that I brought to life within the pages.

ACKNOWLEDGEMENT

I honestly don't think I could have done this without some of the authors I speak to on a regular basis. I wouldn't have known how to set up KDP, or where to find an editor and book cover designer. So to those people, and I hope you know who are you, thank you!

You've all been my own personal cheerleaders and I don't think I could have done this without you.

And to the readers who read my book and gave it a chance. Thank you so much, I hope I didn't disappoint.

ABOUT THE AUTHOR

Powered by tea and sarcasm.

S. Lucas is a self-published indie author, who lives in the UK with their significant other. When they are not writing they can be found either reading, blogging, or sat behind a sewing machine making costumes for various events around the country.

After completing NaNoWriMo for the first time in 2020 with the completed story of Against the Odds, they were set on the track of publishing their very first book.

Look for more books coming in the future.

You can find S Lucas at:

Facebook Page: https://www.facebook.com/authorslucas
Facebook Readers Group: http://www.bit.ly/3rRAgXB
Amazon Author Profile: https://amzn.to/3wuOEbJ
Goodreads: https://bit.ly/3wr4gwW
Instagram: https://www.instagram.com/slucasauthor/
Website : https://slucasauthor.wixsite.com/home

Printed in Great Britain
by Amazon